He brushed his fin of the collar, the hot flutter of Erin's pulse beneath his fingertips sending a jolt of awareness through him.

The contrast of her silken flesh with the unyielding metal collar made her seem all the more fragile and out of place here—like finding a lily blooming in the middle of a minefield.

"Can you cut it off?" she asked.

"I don't think we can risk it," he said. "It looks as if there are wires embedded in the metal and running all the way around. My guess is if we sever one of those the bomb would go off."

She swallowed hard, her eyes as big and dark as a terrified deer's. "What are we going to do?"

He looked away, at the lab equipment arranged neatly on the workbench, at the sparse furnishings and barred windows of the place that had been his prison for the past twelve months. "We need to get out of here," he said.

PhD PROTECTOR

—

CINDI MYERS

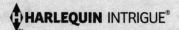

For Vicki and Mike

Recycling programs
for this product may
not exist in your area.

ISBN-13: 978-0-373-75598-1

PhD Protector

Copyright © 2016 by Cynthia Myers

Printed in U.S.A.
www.Harlequin.com

Cindi Myers is the author of more than fifty novels. When she's not crafting new romance plots, she enjoys skiing, gardening, cooking, crafting and daydreaming. A lover of small-town life, she lives with her husband and two spoiled dogs in the Colorado mountains.

Books by Cindi Myers

Harlequin Intrigue

The Men of Search Team Seven

Colorado Crime Scene
Lawman on the Hunt
Christmas Kidnapping
PhD Protector

The Ranger Brigade

The Guardian
Lawman Protection
Colorado Bodyguard
Black Canyon Conspiracy

Rocky Mountain Revenge
Rocky Mountain Rescue

Harlequin Heartwarming

Her Cowboy Soldier
What She'd Do for Love

Visit the Author Profile page at Harlequin.com for more titles.

CAST OF CHARACTERS

Mark Renfro—This top nuclear physicist disappeared almost a year ago and was believed dead. Kidnapped by terrorists, he must pretend to cooperate with them in order to protect his daughter. How can he escape his captors and defeat their plan to detonate a nuclear bomb?

Erin Daniels—The stepdaughter of a terrorist leader wants nothing to do with the group's evil plans, and balks at her stepfather's plans for her to assist his "pet scientist" in building the suitcase nuke he needs. But that scientist is nothing like the man she suspected he'd be, and working with him gives her hope of finding a way out of her messed-up life.

Duane Braeswood—The billionaire terrorist leader believes he can build a better world by first destroying it. He will use anyone and anything to achieve his goals.

Special Agent Luke Renfro—Mark's twin brother, part of the FBI's Search Team Seven, has never stopped looking for his missing brother. He refuses to believe Mark is a terrorist, but can he find him before it's too late?

Mandy Renfro—The five-year old hasn't seen her father in a year, but she never stopped hoping for his return.

Chapter One

What's the worst thing you would do to pro-
tect the ones you love? Would you lie—steal—
even kill?

It was a question from a party game, the
kind you played over beers with a bunch of
buddies, the answers all alcohol-fueled ma-
chismo, backed by the knowledge that you
would never really have to make those kinds
of choices.

Mark Renfro had had to choose. To protect
his daughter, his innocent only child, he had
lied too many times to count, and though he
hadn't stolen or killed—yet—he had joined
with a group of men who were working to kill
thousands, maybe even millions of people.
They called themselves Patriots, but he knew
they were terrorists. They had murdered his

wife, and if Mark didn't do what they wanted, they would kill his daughter, Mandy, as well.

He closed his eyes and rested his forehead against the cool metal of the laboratory hood. Formulas scrolled across his closed eyelids like a particularly boring and technical movie, the complex and intricate calculations of energy transfer and nuclear fusion, pages from textbooks he had read long ago and committed to memory, fragments of scientific papers he had written or read, and columns of computations that lodged in his brain the way phone numbers or the memory of a wonderful meal might take up residence in the brains of others. His photographic memory for all those numbers and calculations had allowed him to breeze though his undergraduate and graduate education and excel at the research that had propelled him to fame and even a little fortune.

All of that worthless, with his wife dead and his daughter far away from him. Amanda had been four when he had last seen her. She'd be five now—a huge chunk of her life he would never get back.

The door to the cabin that had been Mark's prison for over a year burst open, but Mark didn't even jump. The people who held him here were fond of such scare tactics as bursting in unannounced, but he was numb to that all now. "Renfro!" The man Mark knew as Cantrell had a big, booming voice. He was always on the verge of shouting. "We brought you a surprise."

A muffled cry, like that of a wounded animal, made Mark whip around to face Cantrell. But instead of the dog or deer or some other nonhuman victim he had expected to see, he came face-to-face with a furious woman. Her hazel eyes burned with rage and hatred, and the tangle of auburn hair that fell in front of her face couldn't obscure the high cheekbones, patrician nose and delicately pointed chin. She was young—midtwenties, he guessed, with a taut, athletic frame, every muscle straining against the man who held her, a baby-faced goon named Scofield. They had taped her mouth and bound her arms behind her, but still she struggled. So far her efforts had earned her a purpling bruise on one cheek and a torn sleeve on her denim jacket.

Mark half rose from his stool, an old, almost forgotten rage burning deep in his chest. "What do you think you're doing?" he demanded.

"The boss figured you needed some help to speed things along." Cantrell nodded and Scofield shoved the woman forward. She stumbled into Mark and he had to brace his legs and wrap his arms around her to keep them both from crashing into the lab table. "She's your new assistant."

Both men laughed, as if this was the best joke they had heard all year, then they retreated, the locks clicking into place behind them.

Mark still held the woman, though they were both steady on their feet now. It had been so long since he had touched another person, longer still since he had felt a woman's soft, lithe body beneath his hands. She was almost as tall as he was, with small, firm breasts and gently curved hips, and she smelled like flowers and soap and a world very far away from this remote mountain cabin.

She wrenched away from him and stumbled back, staring at him with eyes filled with hatred. He got the feeling she had no more of an idea why she was here than he did. "Turn around and I'll untie your hands," he said. "But you have to promise not to strangle me when I do."

Her eyes made no such promise, but she turned and presented her hands to him. He clipped through the plastic ties with the pair of nail scissors—all his captors would allow him in terms of sharp objects. Though his kidnappers had provided him with a laboratory full of the most up-to-date equipment, they had been very careful to exclude anything that might be used as a weapon.

Ironic, considering the purpose of the laboratory itself.

He pocketed the nail scissors and the woman brought her hands to the front and rubbed them, wincing, then picked at the corners of the tape on her mouth.

"Trust me, the best way is to just rip it off," he said. "It still hurts, but you get it over with quickly."

She hesitated, then did as he suggested and jerked at the silver rectangle of duct tape. "Ah!" she cried out, followed by a string of eloquent curses.

He retreated to his stool in front of the lab bench, fighting the urge to smile. She wouldn't get the joke, wouldn't understand how good it was to hear someone else express the sentiments that had filled his mind for months now. "I'm Mark Renfro," he said. "Who are you?"

"I'm not your assistant," she said, her voice low and rough. Sexy.

She went back to rubbing her wrists, the

movement plumping the cleavage at the scoop neck of her T-shirt. Mark felt a stirring below the belt, his libido rising from the dead, startling him. He had thought himself past such feelings, that part of him burned away by grief and the hopelessness of his situation.

"I didn't request an assistant," he said. "That must have been Cantrell's idea. Or someone higher up the chain of command. I'm sorry they dragged you into this, but I had nothing to do with it."

"You work for them." She moved closer, scanning the array of scientific equipment on the table. "You're their scientist." The disgust in her voice and on her face showed just what she thought of a man who would do such a thing.

"There's a difference between being a slave and an employee. I didn't have any more say about being here than you did." He glanced at her. "Maybe less. You still haven't told me your name."

"Erin. Erin Daniels."

It didn't ring a bell.

"You don't have any idea who I am, do you?" she asked.

He shook his head. "Should I?"

"I don't know. But I would hate for anyone

to associate me with this scum." She began to move about the one-room cabin, taking in the double bedstead in the corner where Mark slept, the open door beside it that led to the single, windowless bathroom, the three-burner gas range and round-topped refrigerator and chipped porcelain sink on the other side of the room, and the table and two chairs that provided the only other seating, aside from the laboratory stool he currently occupied. Her intelligent eyes scanned, assessed and moved on. She tried the sash on the larger of the cabin's two windows.

"They're screwed shut from the outside," he said. "And there's reinforced wire over the glass. If you broke a pane, all you would accomplish would be to let in the cold." He had endured a freezing month right after they took him, when he had tried to cut out one of the panes of glass, in hopes of fashioning a weapon. The glass had shattered and Mark had shivered for weeks before he had persuaded Cantrell that the low temperatures were detrimental to his lab work, and his captors had repaired the pane.

"There must be some way out of here," Erin said, moving to the back door.

"The doors are locked and dead bolted from

the outside, plus there's an armed guard out there at all times. The floor is a concrete slab. The gas is shut off, so the stove doesn't work. They bring in food, unless I'm being punished for something, then I don't eat." They had kept him on short rations for a week after the glass-breaking incident.

"If there's no gas, how do you heat this place?" she asked. "It's in the forties out there today, but it feels fine in here."

"There's electric heat," he said, pointing to the baseboard heating unit along the side wall. "A solar panel charges a battery for that. If the sun doesn't shine for a few days then too bad. I had better learn to like working in the cold." He had spent whole days in bed under the covers in the middle of last winter—he didn't want to think about going through that again.

"How long have you been here?" Her expression was guarded.

"What month is this?" He had tried to keep track at first, then gave up. What did it matter? His captors weren't going to let him leave here alive.

"January," she said. "Today is the ninth."

"Then I've been here fourteen months," he said. The weight of all those months rested on his chest like a concrete block. Crushing.

Erin sank into a chair at the table. "Why?" she asked. "What are you doing here?"

He wanted to say "as little as possible" but he could never be sure the guards weren't listening. He suspected Cantrell or his bosses had the place bugged. She might even be a plant, sent to learn his intentions, though her anger felt very real. Maybe his captors' paranoia was rubbing off on him. "First, tell me your story," he said. "How did you end up here? Are you a scientist?"

"No. I'm a teacher." She straightened a little, as if one of her students might be watching. "I teach math to seventh and eighth graders in Idaho Falls, Idaho."

"Then what are you doing in the middle of nowhere in western Colorado? Do you know anything about the men who brought you here?" What had she done to end up on the wrong side of a group of terrorists like the Patriots?

"Oh, I know about them all right." Her expression grew even more grim. "Their leader is my stepfather."

ERIN KNEW SHE had succeeded in shocking Mark Renfro. Frankly, he had shocked her, too. She had heard so much in the past weeks about the famous scientist who was going to help Duane Braeswood and his group of deranged thugs bring the world to its knees. She had expected him to be like them—a hardened, arrogant braggart whose cruelty showed in knotted muscles and cold expressions. She had been prepared to have to fight him—possibly to the death—to prove she wanted no part of his "mission."

Instead, she had found a thin, weary-looking man in a dirty lab coat, with despair weighting his eyes and slumping his shoulders. He might have been handsome once, before deprivation and grief and whatever other emotions had etched lines at the corners of his eyes and mouth and drained the life from his expression. "You're Braeswood's daughter?" he asked.

"Stepdaughter." At least she didn't have to claim any of that madman's DNA ran through her veins.

Mark sighed and let his hands rest loosely in his lap. "Maybe you'd better start at the beginning," he said.

The beginning. *Once upon a time there was a girl named Erin, who had everything she wanted. Then her father died and her mother made some very poor choices.*

"My mother met a man online when I was

twelve," she said. "My father had died two years before, of liver cancer. She moved back to Idaho to be closer to her family and started hanging out on a survivalist message board. Who knows why?"

"And she met Duane Braeswood through these survivalists?" He nodded. "I guess his ranting might appeal to the more radical factions in that group."

"Do you want me to tell the story or not?"

He looked sheepish. "Sorry. I haven't had anyone to talk to in a while, so I'm rusty at conversation. I won't interrupt again."

She hugged her arms over her chest. "Mom didn't meet Duane on the message board. She met a guy named Amos or Abe or something like that and they dated for a while. She started going to meet ups and gatherings with him and at one of those she met Duane Braeswood." Just remembering the way Duane had come into their lives and taken over made her sick to her stomach. "Among that bunch, he was already a big celebrity. Maybe Mom was flattered by his attention, or impressed by the way he threw money around. Maybe she was just lonely. I don't know."

"Ah, Duane." Mark said the name the way

he might have referred to a notoriously badly behaved public figure.

"Yeah. My mother's second husband." Erin gave him a hard look, ignoring the sympathy in his expression. Maybe he was just a good actor. "Obviously, you know him well."

"No. I've only seen him a few times. He reminds me of a televangelist. One who prefers camo to shiny suits. Though his charm is lost on me, I can see he has a kind of creepy charisma."

"Exactly." She rubbed her arms. "He gave me the creeps from day one, but my mom fell for it. Next thing I knew, she had married him and we moved to this big house with a bunch of other like-minded people, sort of a commune for survivalist types. At first I thought we were just going to stock up on dried food and hunt our own meat and that kind of stuff. I was a kid who wanted to fit in and I thought it might even be fun." Looking back she could see how pathetic she had been, wanting love and approval from her stand-in dad, playing right into his manipulative hands. "As I got older, I figured out he had a more sinister plan."

"The government needs fixing and he's the man to do it," Mark said drily.

She nodded. "He tried to recruit me as one of his loyal followers, but I balked."

"I'm guessing that didn't make you very popular," Mark said.

"I told my mom he was a terrorist, plain and simple. We had a big fight about it. She just couldn't see it." The memory of her mother's rejection still stung. "The day after I graduated high school I left the compound and swore to my mom I wouldn't see her again until she came to her senses and got out of there, too."

Her stomach still knotted when she remembered that day. She had walked out, sure the next time she saw Helen Daniels Braeswood she would be either dead or on the news, arrested for her involvement with some plot of Duane's.

"That must have been tough," Mark said.

"Yeah, well, we didn't speak for four years. Then she called, out of the blue one day, to tell me Duane and the others had left her and moved to Colorado. She sounded worn-out. She asked if she could come stay with me awhile. I was thrilled. I moved her into the house I was renting in Idaho Falls and after a few weeks she was a new woman. She was the mom I had known and loved before. She still refused to admit that Duane was evil. She called him 'misguided but sincere.' She said she had loved him very much but that she was determined to get over him."

Erin fell silent again, remembering all the hope she had had in those months.

"What happened?" Mark prompted after a moment.

"She stayed with me about eighteen months. I thought everything was great. Then one day I came home and found her bags all packed. She said she had had a call from Duane. He had been injured in an accident and he needed her. They were still legally married, so she was going back to him. I went a little crazy. I screamed and yelled and threatened to call the police. She was perfectly calm through the whole thing. She told me one day I would be in love and I would understand. Then she got in a taxi and left."

"How did that lead to you ending up here?" Mark asked.

"I'm getting to that." She took a deep breath, steadying herself. "About six weeks ago, I got a call, from a man who identified himself as Duane's personal assistant. He said he thought I would want to know that my mom was very ill. In fact, she was dying of cancer. She was in hospice and didn't have long and had been asking to see me. He gave me the address he said was for the hospice and suggested I might like to visit her before it was too late." She covered her eyes with her hand, fighting back tears—of grief and rage and shame.

"Did you see her?" Mark asked, his voice gentle.

"She wasn't even sick! It was a trick, to get me to a place where Duane's men could grab me. He showed up, too. He was in a wheelchair, with an oxygen tank. He'd clearly been messed up somehow, but that didn't seem to lessen the power he had over everyone around him. He told me I needed to be punished for upsetting my mother so much, and that he had a job I could do to make up for all the trouble I had caused."

"And his men brought you here."

"First they took me to a fishing camp somewhere in the area, and we stayed there for a few days. I guess they were waiting for some signal from Duane or the stars to align or something. Then they took me to a house in Denver. I stayed there for weeks, in a locked room with the windows blacked out." She glanced around the cabin. "At least this isn't as bad as that."

"Do you know why I'm here?" Mark asked. "What it is that you're supposed to assist me with?"

"Duane always referred to you as his scientist," she said. "A genius he had working for him, I assume on one of his crackpot schemes. What is it this time? A truth serum? Some potion that allows him to see in the dark? A new weapon?"

Mark shifted on his stool and cleared his throat. "You don't know what kind of scientist I am, do you?"

"Duane just told me you were a scientist, and you obviously have some kind of laboratory here."

"I'm a nuclear physicist. Duane Braeswood is holding me prisoner so I can build him a bomb. A nuclear bomb."

Chapter Two

Erin's lovely face reflected all the emotions that had battered at Mark the first time he heard the terrorist leader's plans for him—shock, outrage and finally puzzlement. She glanced around the cabin, with its sparse furnishings and makeshift lab. "How—?"

He didn't let her finish the sentence, but sprang up, grabbed her hand and pulled her toward the refrigerator. "Let me fix you some lunch," he said. "There's cold cuts and stuff in the refrigerator."

She struggled to free herself from his grip, but he held her firmly, pulled open the refrigerator door and leaned in, tugging her alongside him. "We have to be careful what we say," he said, keeping his voice low. "I think the place is bugged."

Her expression tightened and he braced himself for her to dismiss him as a nut. After so many months alone, maybe he was losing it, letting the paranoia take over. But her gaze remained level and she nodded. "That would be just like Duane," she said. "He doesn't trust anyone or take anything for granted."

Mark released her hand and pretended to look through the packages of ham, turkey and cheese on the shelf. "I spend all my time pretending to do the impossible," he mumbled. "Your stepfather wants a nuclear bomb that can be carried around in an oversize suitcase or a backpack, but there's no way that can be done. Certainly not by one man in a facility like this."

"But you've convinced him you can do it." She sounded both horrified and fascinated by the prospect. "Why?"

"As long as I keep working for him, my daughter lives." He grabbed a package of ham and another of cheese and moved away from the refrigerator, back to the table. "There's bread in the cupboard over the sink," he said.

She hesitated, then grabbed the bread and followed him. "You have a daughter?" She kept her voice low, just above a whisper.

"Mandy is five. She was four the last time I saw her."

"Where is she?" Erin's voice rose. "Duane isn't holding her prisoner, too?"

"No, she's safe. She lives with her aunt." At least, he prayed that was still true. Mandy had been with his wife's sister the day Mark left on the hiking trip from which he had never returned. He and Christy had both designated Claire as their chosen guardian for Mandy in their wills, so he had assumed his daughter had stayed with Claire after his disappearance.

"What happened to her mother?" Erin asked.

"She died two months before Duane brought me here." He glanced up from spreading mayonnaise on a slice of bread. "Officially, it was ruled a one-car accident, but someone tampered with her car, I know. Duane wanted to send me a message about the consequences of not cooperating with him."

Sympathy darkened Erin's eyes. "I heard rumors about that kind of thing when I lived with him," she said. "I wanted to believe they weren't true. That no one would be that cruel and manipulative."

"Oh, this is true." When Christy had died, grief and rage at the man responsible consumed him. All these months later, he felt only numb.

"But how did you meet Duane in the first

place?" she asked. "You don't strike me as the prepper type."

"No, I'm not. I had never even heard of Duane Braeswood when he stopped by my office at the University of Colorado one morning about eighteen months ago. He presented himself as a businessman who was interested in providing a grant for research. I was naive enough to be flattered." How many times over the past year had he wished he had had the sense to see through the madman's ruse and refuse to ever speak to him?

"And once he had snared you, he wouldn't let go." She nodded. "He's done it before. He identifies something he wants and then uses whatever means possible to get it."

"At first, he tried to sell me on the scientific advantages of working for him—a private laboratory with top equipment, an endless supply of resources, eventual fame and fortune, and a key role in his new world order." He grimaced. "When that didn't sway me, he turned to threats. I didn't believe him. I thought he was a crackpot but harmless. I found out too late that he was anything but."

"I'm sorry about your wife," Erin said, all the hardness gone from her voice.

"Thank you." He swallowed, regaining his

composure. "When he threatened my daughter next, I knew I didn't have any choice but to cooperate."

"So now you're trying to do the impossible."

"I'm the best—or one of the best—nuclear physicists in the country." He raised his voice for the benefit of anyone who might be listening in. "The organization supplies me with anything I need, from high-grade uranium ore to the most sophisticated equipment. It's only a matter of time." He met her eyes, letting her know he was lying through his teeth.

"And I'm supposed to help you." She stared down at her completed sandwich. "I don't know the first thing about nuclear physics."

"You're a math teacher. That should come in handy. You can help me with my calculations."

She looked around the cabin again. "You don't have a computer?"

He shook his head.

"And I don't see any books. Don't you need reference materials? Formulas?"

He tapped the side of his head. "It's all in here." He almost laughed at the skepticism that was so plain on her face. "No, really. I have a photographic memory. I've memorized all the textbooks and formulas and manuals. Once I read something, I remember it. Some of my colleagues thought I was a freak, but it made me the perfect candidate for Duane's little project." Finding out how thoroughly the Patriots' leader had vetted him had made Mark feel even more vulnerable and helpless, as if there was nowhere to hide from Duane's reach.

"I thought photographic memories were something people made up for movies and books," she said.

"No, it's a real phenomenon. Something to do with how the person's brain is wired. There may even be a genetic component in this case. My mother had perfect pitch. My twin brother never forgets a face."

"You have a twin?"

"Yes. Luke is an FBI agent. He's part of a special task force composed of people like him—super-recognizers who never forget a face."

"An FB—" She shook her head. "Then Duane is an idiot—and I don't care who hears me say that."

"Duane believes he's untouchable," Mark said. And maybe he was. The man had managed to get away with murder—literally—for a while now. "I know Luke is looking for me," he continued. "But Duane is hunting him, too.

He's made it known he'll pay a big bonus to anyone who kills a Fed."

"He bragged about it to me, too."

He studied her, wishing he could decipher people as easily as he could chemical formulas. Was she telling the truth about how she had ended up here, or was this merely one more way for Braeswood and his bunch to mess with Mark's mind? "Why did he send you here, really?" he asked, leaning toward her. "I don't need an assistant for this project. Are you here to spy on me? Will you report back to him everything I've said?" He ought to be afraid of those consequences, but after all this time trapped here with no way out he would welcome a bullet to end it all.

"You really think I would work for people like them? That I could believe in their sick plots or condone anything they do?" She shoved the sandwich away and glared at him, cheeks flushed, eyes blazing.

"Accusing me isn't the same as denial," he pointed out.

"No! I don't want anything to do with those monsters. And I don't want anything to do with you." She stalked away and sat on the end of the unmade bed, her back to him.

Even from across the room, he imagined the

heat of her anger washing over him. He welcomed the warmth, the intensity of the emotion, the *life* in her. For so long now—before they had even brought him here, since Christy's death—he had felt cold and hollow inside, more robot than man. Only his daughter had been able to stir him, her tiny breath able to coax sparks from the few coals of life left inside him.

Then she was gone and the fire had died altogether. He had gone through the motions of living, but had felt nothing.

Now Erin was here, all fiery anger and glowing life, making him remember things—hatred and hunger and sex. Somehow being near a woman, after so many months with only the company of other men, reminded him of his own humanity. He wasn't dead after all, but he didn't know if that knowledge was good or bad. Living meant feeling—risking and caring and hurting. All things he had told himself he couldn't afford to do again.

ERIN ENVIED MARK'S COMPOSURE. She couldn't sit still, agitation driving her to pace. She had lived with fear for so long it was part of her makeup now, like the color of her hair or the shape of her face. Even years after she had left the family compound she continued to look over her shoulder, expecting her stepfather to make good on all the threats he had hurled at her when she'd walked away from him. Duane had a need to control situations and people. If you thwarted him, you could expect to be punished.

He had bided his time, but he had finally exacted his revenge, though she still wasn't sure of his final plans for her. She kept expecting his thugs to come back for her—to tie her up again and tell her there had been a change of plans, that this remote cabin wasn't her real destination. This place was too bizarre, even for Duane. Did he really believe he could build a nuclear bomb in a place like this? With a scientist who didn't even bother to look at a book?

She risked a glance at Mark, who had returned to work at the lab table. He wore goggles and a mask and was working with his hands in heavy gloves, manipulating something inside a large glass box. Maybe the protective gear was because the material in that box was radioactive. She wrapped her arms around her shoulders to ward off a sudden chill.

She couldn't figure Mark out. The story he had told her—about his wife and little girl—

was horrifying. She was pretty sure Duane had killed other people, so why not Mark's wife? But how could Mark be so calm about his situation? She had spent every waking moment for the last six weeks trying to figure out how to escape from her captors. She had almost succeeded twice—she still winced, remembering the beatings she'd received when she had been caught. But Duane hadn't let them kill her or rape her or otherwise harm her. She had thought he drew the line there out of consideration for her mother, but now she wondered if it was because he had other plans for her. Plans that included the enigmatic Mark Renfro.

Her stomach growled. The sandwich she had made earlier still sat on the kitchen counter, so she retrieved it and took it to the table to eat. Mark glanced up from his work. "They usually bring dinner by now," he said. "Since they haven't, we may have to make do with cold cuts."

She shrugged. She didn't want to talk to him, didn't want to get any closer to him, but curiosity—and maybe loneliness—weakened her resolve. "What are you doing?" she asked.

"I'm using a solvent to extract pure uranium from powdered ore," he said. "The process takes a couple of days, but there's a lot of high-grade ore in this area. I think that's why Duane was interested in the property in the first place. Some things I've overheard make me think he hasn't owned the place long—that he acquired it specifically for this purpose. The remote location suits his purposes well, too."

"I still don't understand how you convinced Duane you could make a bomb out here," she said. "He's insane, but he isn't stupid."

He removed his hands from the box, pulled down the mask and pushed up the goggles and faced her. "I didn't convince him of anything. He decided it could be done and chose me to do it."

"But what made him think it was even possible?" she asked. "Don't you need, I don't know, a particle accelerator or something like that?"

He chuckled. "Actually, in the 1960s, three physics students working in a small laboratory were able to design a functional bomb. The United States government paid them to make the attempt. They wanted to see if it was possible for a few people with a limited amount of knowledge and not a lot of sophisticated equipment—a situation that might crop up in an underdeveloped country, for example—to make a nuclear weapon. Turned out they could. The government called it the Nth Country Experiment. You can read about it online if you're interested. And in 1994 a teenage Eagle Scout built a nuclear reactor in his backyard, using materials he found around the house."

"So you really could build a bomb?" The idea made her skin crawl.

"I'm sure I could, given enough time and the right materials." He scrawled something on a piece of paper and passed it over to her. *In case anyone is listening—building a bomb isn't the problem. Building one small enough for one person to carry around inconspicuously is.*

She nodded and crumpled the paper, holding it tight in her clenched fist. "I still don't see how I can help you."

"Perhaps you're merely here to boost my morale."

She narrowed her eyes. "Don't get any ideas."

He frowned. "I only meant that having someone to talk to is a nice change."

Right. Maybe she had grown too accustomed to the company of Duane's goons who, despite their boss's orders not to lay a hand on her, spent plenty of time leering and making lewd remarks. "How have you kept from going crazy, alone here for so many months?" she asked.

"I try not to think about it too much," he said. "And I focus on the work." He turned back to the lab equipment.

She stared at his back for a long while, then stood and walked to the window. He could focus on work all he wanted, but she was going to focus on finding a way out of here.

In different circumstances, she might have enjoyed the view out this window. The cabin sat on a slight rise at the edge of a valley. Feathery junipers and piñon pines dotted the rocky ground amid a thick blanket of snow. A few hundred yards beyond the cabin the land fell away in a steep precipice. Across from this gorge rose red rock mountains, the peaks cloaked in white, the setting sun painting the sky in brilliant pinks and golds. How ironic that such a peaceful-seeming place could be the source of potentially great destruction.

A cloud of white off in the distance, moving in their direction, caught her attention. "I think someone's coming," she said.

Mark was by her side within seconds. "That looks like Duane's entourage," he said, as three black Humvees slowly made their way up the narrow, rutted track. A guard who must have been seated on the other side of the door rose and walked to the edge of the narrow porch, an automatic rifle cradled in his arms. When the vehicles stopped in front of the cabin, the guard snapped off a salute.

Erin didn't even realize she had backed away from the window until she bumped into Mark. He rested one hand on her shoulder, steadying her, and she fought the urge to lean into him. She didn't even know the man, and didn't fully trust him, yet she felt safer with him than with any of those on the other side of the door.

Men piled out of the first and third vehicles, all dressed in camo and bristling with weapons. One man unpacked a wheelchair and set it up next to the middle vehicle, while another man opened the back door of this Hummer, leaned in and lifted out Duane Braeswood.

Mark sucked in his breath. "Is that really Duane?" he asked. "What happened to him?"

Instead of camo, Duane wore a black suit and turtleneck. His thin body was twisted and hunched, and tubes trailed from his nostrils to an oxygen tank that one of his goons hooked to the back of the wheelchair.

"You didn't know?" She had been shocked, too, the first time she saw this sick, diminished version of her stepfather. But he was diminished in physical stature only. His spirit had struck her as stronger than ever.

"I haven't seen him in almost a year," Mark said.

"Don't let his appearance fool you. He isn't weak." Despite his disability, the man in the wheelchair radiated power, with every man out there focused on him.

The group headed for the cabin, two of the men lifting the wheelchair, with Duane in it, onto the porch. Mark pulled Erin into the middle of the room as locks snicked and the door opened.

She forced herself to look at her stepfather, to meet the blue eyes that burned feverishly in his withered face. "Erin, dear." The sound of her name on his lips made her flinch. "Your mother sends her greetings."

She bit back a curse, aware of the guards looming on either side of him. She had found out the hard way what they thought of any slur on the man they viewed almost as a religious figure. "How is my mother?" she asked, because she wanted desperately to know, though she knew Duane would tell her the truth only if it suited him.

"Helen is fine." He rolled his chair toward the lab. "Renfro!" The strident voice seemed incongruous coming from such a weakened frame. "What progress have you made?"

Mark walked to the workbench, unhurried, his hands in the pockets of his lab coat, the picture of the singularly focused genius who couldn't be bothered to worry about anything outside of his work. "I've almost perfected the refining process," he said. "And I'm accumulating the quantity of uranium I'll need for the project."

"You need to finish within a week," Duane said.

Mark's expression didn't change. If anything, he looked even more bored, eyes hooded, his expression guarded. "I can't promise that. The process takes as long as it takes. I can't change physical laws."

Erin didn't see any signal from Duane, but he must have given one. Without warning, two men seized her arms, while a third forced her head back.

"Leave her alone!" Mark shouted, all semblance of boredom vanished, but the fourth guard held him back.

Erin tried to struggle, terrified her captors intended to cut her throat. But the two men who held her remained immobile, impervious to her kicks and shouts. A third man wrapped something hard and cold around her throat. She heard a click, and all three men suddenly released her.

"I wouldn't make any sudden movements if I were you, Erin." Duane's voice had its usual smooth cadence. "The mechanism in your new necklace is fairly sensitive."

The three goons stepped back and Erin grabbed at her throat, grasping the thick metal collar now fastened there. The edges chafed her skin and the weight of it dragged at her. "What have you done to me?" she demanded.

"You're wearing an explosive device," Duane said, as calmly as if he had been commenting on the weather. "It has a timer, and is set to go off exactly one week from today." He turned to Mark. "You deliver the product as promised by then and we will remove the collar."

"Why such a hurry now?" Mark asked. "You've waited all these months, why not a few more to make sure things are done correctly?"

"I'm done with waiting." Duane's voice was strident, his face red with strain. "You will have the device for me in a week."

"And if I don't?"

"Then the bomb goes off and you both die."

Chapter Three

Mark stared at the man in the wheelchair. The eyes that looked back at him were as cold and untroubled as a mountain lake. Erin had been right—whatever physical ailment had reduced Duane to a husk of his former self, it hadn't diminished his madness. A man with eyes like that might very well kill his own stepdaughter just to make a point. But delivering what Duane wanted within a week—or even within a year—was impossible. Mark chose his words carefully, wary of upsetting his kidnapper more. "Mr. Braeswood, building a…an apparatus such as you require isn't like baking a cake. I can't just throw a bunch of ingredients together and come up with a viable product. I need time and—"

"You've had time," Braeswood snapped. "If

I don't have what I want in one week, you both die."

And even if I could deliver your bomb, we would still die, Mark thought. Duane wouldn't leave any witnesses to his plans. "You're asking for the impossible," he said.

"You'll have your bomb. Next week!" Despite the constricting collar Erin turned her head to face Braeswood. "Mark is being a typical scientist—overly cautious. He was telling me earlier that he's almost ready to assemble it. With both of us working together I know we can meet your deadline."

"Erin." Mark sent her a warning look.

Her gaze burned into him, pleading with him to go along with her lie. Her terror swamped him. Maybe he would feel the same if he had a bomb at his throat. "Sure," he said, dropping his gaze to the floor. "There's still some work I need to do...with the plutonium-catalyst ratios." There was no such thing, but Mark had learned that Braeswood appreciated it when he threw around scientific jargon.

"Excellent." Braeswood's voice sounded much stronger than he looked. Floorboards creaked as he turned his chair and rolled back to the door. "I'll see you next week, then."

"You can't just leave me like this!" Erin's voice rose, on the edge of panic.

"So impatient." Braeswood regarded her coolly. "You were that way as a child, too, never content to wait for a reward, no matter how hard I tried to teach you. I would have hoped that maturity would have curbed that unfortunate character trait, but I see it has not. This should be a good lesson for you." He nodded to his henchmen and one opened the door while two others hoisted the chair.

The locks snapped into place again after the door closed behind the entourage. Car doors slammed, engines growled and the pop of tires on gravel gradually faded away.

Erin sank into one of the kitchen chairs, as if her legs would no longer support her, her hands clutching the collar. "I can't believe this is happening," she moaned.

Mark's hands knotted into fists and his heart hammered, emotion rocking him back on his heels. He recognized rage—something he hadn't felt, something he hadn't allowed himself to feel, in months. The intensity of the feelings caught him off guard. He was furious with Braeswood and his men, but also with himself. Why hadn't he done something to stop them? Why hadn't he protected Erin?

And what was he going to do to help her now? He may have given up on life, but she deserved to live.

He pulled his hands from his pockets and moved to her side. "Can I take a look at the collar?" he asked.

She dropped her hands to her lap and looked up at him. "Do you know anything about disarming bombs?"

"Not a thing, unfortunately." He studied the collar, which was gold colored—plated, he imagined, with platinum or aluminum or some other sturdier alloy beneath. About three inches wide, it fastened at the back with a locking mechanism similar to a seat belt, the halves fitting tightly together. The explosive device sat front and center, the size of a pack of playing cards, comprised of wires and button batteries and a glob of yellowish plastic he suspected was the explosive. Who had made this horrible yet ingenious device for Duane? Did he have a combination jeweler-explosives expert in the ranks of his followers? Or was he holding another man prisoner, compelling him by threat or force to do Duane's malevolent bidding?

Mark brushed his fingers along the sides of the collar, the hot flutter of Erin's pulse be-

neath his fingertips sending a jolt of awareness through him. The contrast of her silken
flesh with the unyielding metal made her seem
all the more fragile and out of place here—
like finding a lily blooming in the middle of
a minefield.

"Can you cut it off?" she asked.

"I don't think we can risk it," he said. "It
looks as if there are wires embedded in the
metal and running all the way around. My
guess is if we sever one of those the bomb
would go off."

She swallowed hard, her eyes as big and
dark as a terrified deer's. "What are we going
to do?"

He looked away, at the lab equipment arranged neatly on the workbench, at the sparse
furnishings and barred windows of the place
that had been his prison for the past fourteen
months. "We need to get out of here," he said.
"We need to get you to someplace with people who know how to disarm something like
this." The FBI had experts who could deal with
this kind of thing. If he could get to Luke, his
brother would know what to do.

"How are we going to get away?" she asked.

If he knew that, he would have left months
ago. Escaping from the cabin might not even

be the most difficult challenge. Once they were free, they would have to cross miles of wilderness in freezing weather before they could even reach a road, or a telephone they could use to summon help. "I don't know." He dropped into the chair across from her. "I tried everything I could think of when I first got here. I was always caught." Caught and punished. He closed his eyes. He understood now that it wasn't merely confinement that wore down prisoners—it was the utter helplessness, the loss of control over even the simplest aspects of life.

"How many guards are there?" she asked.

"Two at a time—one on the front door and one on the back. They work eight-hour shifts, so that means six men a day, plus two others that rotate in and out when one of the others needs to take a day off. They're armed with semiautomatic rifles and unlike the men in books and movies, they don't fall asleep or get distracted." He had spent many hours in the early days of his captivity studying his guards and trying to learn their patterns and spot any weaknesses. Unfortunately, he hadn't identified any of the latter.

"So Duane has eight men stationed somewhere near here, but only two of them are up here at a time," she said. "There are two of us now. That evens the odds." She sounded stronger, and some of the color had returned to her face.

"Except we're not armed," he said. "And where do we go when we do get out of here? We're miles from any major road, we don't have a map and, in case you haven't noticed, there's snow out there."

"I'd rather freeze to death in the mountains than sit here waiting to be blown up."

Until she showed up, Mark would have opted for sitting. Truth was, he had given up months ago. Without his wife, without his daughter or his work, he had nothing to live for. But Erin was young. Not that much younger than him in terms of years, but she was so full of life. She had every reason to avoid death.

"Why is Duane doing all this now?" he asked. "Why lure you back to him after years away? Why demand a bomb in a week after I've been working on it over a year? He hasn't shown any sign of impatience with the project before now."

"Maybe he's tired of paying for all the man power needed to keep you up here," she said.

"He hasn't balked at paying the money before. Has something happened to make him worried about finances?"

She shook her head. "Duane's grandfather was some kind of robber baron who made a killing in insurance in the twenties. Apparently, even the Depression didn't touch his fortune. His father parlayed those millions into billions with a string of tech companies. Duane apparently inherited their knack for business and invested in everything from highways to high tech to fund his more nefarious activities—the actual source of the money all neatly hidden in various shell companies and shadow corporations. Add to that the donations he receives from people who support his cause and he's got an endless supply of bucks. All this—" she swept her hand around the lab "—probably only qualifies as a footnote on a spreadsheet somewhere."

"If it's not money, what else is driving him?" Mark asked. "Has something happened on the world scene to make him think now is the best time to strike? I haven't heard a news report in the last year, so we could be ruled by Martians right now and I wouldn't know it." He'd been like a castaway on a deserted island. He had told himself he didn't miss knowing what was going on in the rest of the world, but now that Erin was with him, he fought the urge to bombard her with questions: *Who was president of Russia these days? What was the dollar worth? What was the hottest tech gadget? Who was hosting the next Olympic Games? Who'd won the World Series?*

But he had held back, and now, with that horrible collar around her neck, didn't seem the time to worry about trivialities.

"There's nothing much new in the world situation that would have set him off," she said. "Though maybe his accident has him thinking about his mortality, and that's given him this sense of urgency."

"What kind of accident?" Mark asked. "I'll admit I was shocked by his appearance this afternoon—I haven't seen him in months. I thought maybe he had cancer or something."

"I'm not sure what is wrong with him, but I don't think it's cancer," she said. "I only heard bits and pieces of the story from my mom or from things people said when they didn't know I was listening. It's something to do with the FBI—he was injured when they tried to capture him or something like that. It's one of the reasons he hates them so much."

"Did you overhear anything else interesting, about Duane or his plans?"

"There was some rumor about a power struggle between Duane and his second in command, a man named Roland Chambers. He lived with us for a while when I was a teenager and he practically worshipped Duane, so I don't know how much truth there was to the rumors that he was trying to take over after Duane was injured. But Roland was killed last month, so Duane doesn't have to worry about him anymore."

"So no money problems, no political upheaval and no rival." Mark ticked off the possible reasons for Duane's sudden change of plans. "Maybe you're right and it is a mortality thing. I guess it doesn't matter why he's putting the pressure on us, only that he is."

"We've got to find a way out of here," she said.

"If you think of a plan, I'll try it."

She surprised him once more by leaning over and gripping his hand. "We'll think of something," she said.

Her conviction both stunned and moved him. A wave of emotion—regret, longing, even hope—welled up in him, so strong he had to look away for fear of betraying his weakness. Five hours ago he had been contemplating ways to end his life. Now, thanks to Erin,

he was desperate to hang on to all the time he
had left—to not only survive, but to live.

THE COLLAR WASN'T tight enough to choke her,
Erin reminded herself, fighting the panic that
lurked at the very edge of consciousness. But
the thick metal band felt like Duane's hands
around her throat, threatening to squeeze the
life from her.

Mark had returned to his workbench, bend-
ing over his experiments as if the previous hour
hadn't happened. She supposed his work was
his escape, the way some people lost themselves in television shows or books. But she
had no escape, only a hyperawareness of the
weight around her throat and the fear that a
wrong move could set off the bomb that would
tear her to pieces. She had lived with fear so
long she thought she had grown accustomed
to it, but Duane had found a way to ratchet up
the terror until it was almost unbearable.

She replayed every conversation she had had
with him since she had returned to his sphere
of influence—not so much conversations as
arguments and debates, often exchanged at
top volume while her mother hovered nearby,
a diminutive referee prepared to throw her-

self between the opponents should they come to blows.

Erin's refusal to follow Duane's dictates or believe in his worldview had always annoyed and even angered her stepfather. As a teen, his attitude had only egged her on. As an adult, she saw a hatred she hadn't noticed before, lurking beneath the surface ranting. Maybe this whole charade with the kidnapping and the collar was an elaborate revenge plot. Maybe she was the primary target of Duane's latest ultimatum, not Mark and his bomb-building assignment. He was collateral damage incurred along the way.

Engrossed in his work, Mark didn't even seem aware she was in the room. She studied him, determined to distract herself from thinking any more about the collar. He was a fairly tall man—over six feet, his frame lanky beneath the loose-fitting lab coat. His dark hair just touched his collar, the cut uneven, as if he had done it himself with the pair of nail scissors. The thought of him struggling to remain well-groomed despite the direness of his situation touched her.

He had probably shaved this morning, but now dark stubble shadowed his jaw, sharpening his features and making him look less like a scientist and more like an outlaw, or a fugitive on the run.

She wanted to be on the run, but the wire mesh on the windows and the guards at the doors blocked their escape. She studied the ceiling. If they could find a way to climb up onto the roof, could they jump off and flee before the guards noticed? But the cabin didn't appear to have an attic, and she doubted they had tools capable of sawing through the metal roofing. The concrete beneath the floor meant tunneling wasn't an option.

She sighed and closed her eyes, determined not to give in to the tears that threatened.

"It's getting dark."

Mark's voice startled her. She opened her eyes, surprised to note the landscape around the cabin was no longer visible through the windows.

"Darkness comes early at this elevation, this time of year," Mark said. "Are you hungry? You should try to eat." He moved from the workbench to the refrigerator and began pulling out cold cuts. "I'll make sandwiches."

"I couldn't eat," she said, but he kept assembling bread and ham and cheese.

He set a sandwich and a bottle of water in front of her and took the chair across from her. She stared at the food and shook her head. "I couldn't."

He looked down at his own plate, then pushed it away. "Yeah. I don't have much of an appetite, either. Maybe we should just call it a night. The batteries drain pretty fast once the sun goes down, so I've gotten in the habit of retiring early. Maybe in the morning we'll think with clearer heads."

She looked at the double bed with its tangle of sheets and blankets. "I don't think I could sleep," she said.

"Take the bed," he said. "I'll stretch out on the floor."

"That's ridiculous. I won't take your bed."

His expression grew stubborn. "Call me old-fashioned, but I'm not going to rest in comfort while you try to make do on the floor."

"Then we'll share the bed." She looked him in the eye, striving for a calm she didn't feel. "We're adults. We can do that. Under the circumstances, it's ridiculous to be prudish about something like this. There's only one bed and two of us, so we should make the best of it."

"All right. Suit yourself." He stood and returned their leftovers to the refrigerator, then removed the lab coat and draped it over the stool at his workbench.

Erin blinked. The baggy coat had hid the outline of his body. Beneath it he wore a blue flannel shirt that stretched across lean but muscular shoulders, and canvas hiking pants that hugged a narrow waist and decidedly attractive backside.

He turned and caught her staring at him. "Is something wrong?" he asked.

She shook her head, fighting to hold back a blush. "I was just…lost in thought." The thought that there was more to the depressed scientist than she had first surmised.

They moved to the bed. The metal frame was shoved into the corner. "I'll take the outside," she said, not wanting to be trapped between him and the wall.

"All right." He removed his shoes, then, still wearing his pants and shirt, slid under the covers and rolled over to face the wall, his back to her.

She sat on the side of the bed and slipped out of her own shoes, then switched off the lamp and lay back on top of the blankets. The metal collar rubbed against the underside of her chin and she tried not to think of the possibility that she might roll over in sleep and put pressure on the wrong wire or something…

She closed her eyes and tried to focus on her

breathing—eight slow counts in, eight slow counts out. A friend who taught yoga had assured her that this was a surefire technique for releasing tension and falling asleep.

On the first count of eight Mark shifted, the movement rocking the bed and banishing all thoughts of achieving calm. The heat of him caressed her skin and she sensed the shape of him only inches from her, the jut of his shoulders, the long line of his spine, the length of his legs. The memory of him brushing his fingertips along her throat made her heart speed up and her breath catch. Not because she could ever be attracted to a man like Mark Renfro— a man still in mourning for his dead wife and lost child, a man whose eyes held a despair that tore at her. She was reacting this way only because it had been a long time since she had slept with a man. A long time since she had lived in the same house with anyone else. She had avoided close relationships, fearful of exposing anyone else to Duane's manipulations and hate. Duane controlled people by threatening those they loved, as he had done with Mark. Avoiding love protected other people, but it was also a way of protecting herself.

But that kind of life was lonely, and clearly, Erin was paying for that now. She told herself simple human contact, not sexual attraction, had set her heart pounding and her skin heating over Mark's proximity.

She took a cue from him and rolled over to put her back to him, clinging to the side of the bed and trying to ignore the weight of the bomb collar against her throat. She closed her eyes and allowed the tears to wet her lashes and slide down her cheeks as she prayed for sleep to take her.

MARK LAY AWAKE deep into the night, stretched out rigid on the mattress, the events of the day playing and replaying behind his closed eyelids. The sudden appearance of Erin, followed by Duane's visit and his homicidal ultimatum, unsettled him more than he would have thought possible, like a trumpet blast disrupting the white noise of the lab, or a slash of vivid crimson across a black-and-white photo.

When sleep finally pulled him under, he dreamed restless, confusing vignettes: he was at a birthday party for four-year-old Mandy, Christy leaning forward, cheeks puffed out, helping her daughter blow out the candles on the cake. He saw Christy in the kitchen, long blond hair partially covered by a pink bandanna, a smudge of flour on one cheek, brows drawn together in fierce concentration as she studied the directions in a cookbook.

Then Christy was in bed beside him, the thin straps of her nightgown slipping off her shoulders, a warm smile deepening the dimple in one cheek as she pulled him to her. She was so incredibly warm and soft, skin as fine as silk as he glided his hands over her shoulders, turning her around and pulling her back tight against him, the curve of her bottom snugged against the hard length of his arousal.

He cupped her breast, the beaded nipple nuzzling into his palm. She murmured and shifted, then made a sound of alarm and jerked away.

Mark stared into a pair of wide feminine eyes—not blue like Christy's, but the gold-green hazel of the forest floor. Erin's eyes, filled with accusations and questions.

Chapter Four

Erin had surfaced from a stupor of exhaustion to luxurious warmth—the warmth of a firm male body pressed to hers, strong hands caressing her. She smiled, and snuggled into the heat of him, this dream man whose fingers played across her skin as if she was precious to him. She gave a purr of satisfaction as he cupped her breast, a glow building within her. Yes. How long had it been since she had felt so aroused—so cherished?

The question intruded into the fantasy, demanding an answer, summoning reality. Opening her eyes, she stared at the lab equipment on a counter across from her, shadowed in the dim light of early dawn filtering through the mesh-covered windows of the cabin. Emotions tumbled over her like falling debris—confusion, anger, fear—topped off by the knowledge that whoever had his hands on her and his body against her, it wasn't a lover, because she hadn't had one of those in a long time.

Fear lanced through her as she pulled out of his grasp and rolled onto her back to stare into the troubled face of Mark Renfro. "I'm sorry." He held up his hands, like a robber caught reaching into the till. "I didn't mean… I was dreaming… I'm sorry."

She did a quick check as her initial panic receded—they were both still dressed, nothing out of place. Mark looked so horrified she had to believe him. After all, she had been dreaming, too, and the dream hadn't been at all unpleasant. "It's okay." She managed a smile. "Nothing really happened. I guess this just proves you're human."

He rose up on one elbow and wiped his hand over his face. "Nothing like this has ever happened to me before."

"I think we could both say that about pretty much everything these days." She sat up and hugged her knees to her chest. "Must have been a nice dream, huh?"

The room had lightened enough to show the flush of color on his cheeks that made him look much younger and quite endearing. "It's okay," she said again. "The mind is a funny thing. The subconscious can throw up the oddest stuff when you least expect it."

He sat up also, then leaned over and pulled a small transistor radio from beneath the bed and switched it on. The white noise of static surrounded them. "I read once that was one way to make it tougher for a hidden microphone to pick up conversation." He shrugged. "I don't know if it's true or not, but it doesn't hurt to be careful."

"Where did you get that?" she asked.

"I found it under the bed after I had been here a couple of weeks. I guess whoever owned the cabin before left it behind." He leaned back against the iron bedstead. "I don't suppose your subconscious has come up with a way to get us out of here?"

She touched the collar at her neck, the metal smooth and heavy and deadly. Then she glanced at the array of lab equipment. "There must be something there we can use as a weapon," she said. "I mean, you're supposed to be building a bomb. So you must have some dangerous stuff."

"Radioactive material is potentially deadly," he said. "But by itself it doesn't kill or disable instantly, like a bullet or a knife. If we threatened the guards with a chunk of radioactive rock, they would just shoot us."

"What else have you got? Chemicals?"

"I have some solvents, a couple of acids—"

"That's it." She leaned toward him. "Throw acid on someone and you could certainly disable them."

"But they have to get close enough for you to be sure you don't miss," he said. "You might take out one guard that way, but not both of them."

She mulled over this problem. "I could create a distraction. Something they would both have to respond to. You could douse them with acid and we could make a run for it."

He didn't automatically dismiss the plan, which she considered a positive sign. "What kind of distraction?"

"I don't know. It would have to be something that would bring them inside. What about a fire? Or a minor explosion in the lab?"

"I tried that the second week I was here. One of them stuck his head in and told me if I burned the place down with me in it, I would save them all a lot of trouble. I ruined my only sweater putting out the blaze."

"I could scream rape."

He shook his head. "From what I've seen

of this bunch, they'd either want to watch or participate."

She cringed. "Right. Bad idea." She rubbed a finger under the collar. "If I told them something was wrong with this, they would probably want to keep their distance." She looked around the cabin. "What do they care about in here?"

"Nothing," he said. "The only time they set foot inside is to bring food, and then one of them keeps his gun on me while the other one sets the bags on the table. The whole process takes about three minutes."

"So you've been practically living in solitary confinement." No wonder he was depressed.

"I would rather be by myself than have anything to do with people like them," he said. "Killers who justify what they do with a pretense of saving the country from itself."

"So we'll have to make our move when they bring the food," she said. "When do they usually bring it?"

"Midafternoon. I thought they were making a delivery when they brought you."

"Do they come every day?"

"No. Three or four times a week."

"Next time they come we won't make our move, but we'll watch and see if we can spot any weak points. Have you ever seen any other women up here?"

"Never."

"I've seen a few hanging around Duane's compound—a few wives and girlfriends of the men who follow him. Maybe a few of the women are followers, too. But there's never any female muscle. That runs counter to all those old-fashioned values they like to espouse."

"What are you getting at?" he asked.

"These guys aren't around women a lot," she said. "They don't know how to handle them."

"They don't have any problem killing women," he said, and she wondered if he was thinking of his dead wife.

Her stomach knotted. "I don't intend to let them kill me if I can help it. But I was thinking if I got a little hysterical it might throw them off balance long enough for you to douse them with the acid."

"That's a lot of *if*s."

"The alternative is sitting here and waiting to be blown up. I would rather take the risk."

"And what happens after that?" he asked. "After we get outside? I don't even know where we are. Do you?"

"No. But there is a road leading up here, and

if we head down the mountain and keep walking, we're bound to eventually reach a house or a highway or someone who can help us." She angled her body toward him. "We can gather supplies to take with us—food and water and blankets. When we get to a phone we can call your brother the FBI agent."

"The guards will come after us. It won't be as simple as walking away from here."

"If we disable both guards on duty, we'll have a head start. I'll admit it won't be easy, but if we don't at least try it, we'll die for sure."

He let out a long breath. "You're right." His eyes met hers, a strength in them she hadn't seen before. "We'll do it."

ERIN'S DETERMINATION TO escape kindled a fire in Mark. He felt like a man awakening after a long sleep, dormant emotions coming to life once more. Last night's erotic dream was just one more sign of his reawakening. When he had first come to the cabin, he had fought, but weeks of isolation and torture and no success from his efforts had left him listless and numb. The sight of the beautiful woman sentenced to death by the bomb around her throat hit him like an injection of adrenaline.

"I did an inventory of the lab equipment and

supplies," he told Erin as they ate lunch—the last of the sandwich fixings—that afternoon. She had spent the morning looking out the windows, not speaking. Maybe the direness of their situation was sinking in.

"How do you replenish your supplies?" she asked. She lifted the top slice of bread on her turkey sandwich and frowned at the grayish meat inside.

"I make a list and give it to the guard who delivers the food." Mark bit into his own sandwich. After his first weeks here he had learned to eat when food was offered, since he could never be sure when the next meal would arrive. "I'm pretty well stocked right now, but I need more nitric acid. I use it to process the plutonium." Any chemist would recognize this as a gross oversimplification of what he did, but the guards didn't strike him as chemistry majors.

"So you think they'll bring more food this afternoon?" she asked.

"I hope so. We need more food since there are two of us now."

"It must be pretty boring for the guards," she said. "I've been watching them all morning and they just walk around the cabin all day. What do they do when it snows, or at night?"

"There's someone on guard all the time," he

said. "Sometimes they build a fire in winter, and they have a trailer parked nearby, where they can take turns warming up."

He could almost read her thoughts. She was thinking if they could get out of here at a time when only one guard was outside, they would have a better chance of getting away.

"They keep the doors locked from the outside," he reminded her.

She nodded, still thoughtful.

The crunch of tires on ice alerted them to new arrivals. "This might be our dinner," he said, standing.

She stood also, and together they faced the door. A car door slammed, locks turned and the door swung open to reveal a guard Mark had named Tank—a thick-muscled, broad-shouldered guy with a shaved head, a gold front tooth and a permanent scowl. The floor shook as he strode toward them, two plastic grocery bags looped over one hand, the other balled into a fist at his side.

A second guard—a wiry black man with a thin mustache—positioned himself by the door, a semiautomatic rifle held across his chest. He glanced at Mark, then his gaze fixed on Erin and one corner of his mouth lifted in a sneer. She moved a little closer to Mark, her breath shallow, skin pale. He wanted to put out a hand to steady her, maybe squeeze her shoulder to reassure her, but doing anything to draw attention to her felt like the wrong move.

Tank set the grocery bags on the table, the cans and bottles inside rattling. At this point, he usually turned and shuffled out, but this afternoon was different. He moved toward Erin, who shrank back.

"I'm supposed to check your collar," he said, and took hold of her arm, dragging her toward him.

She stood rigid, jaw clamped shut, as he ran one thick finger under the edge of the metal collar. The other hand slid down her arm to cup her breast. "Yeah," he murmured. "Nice."

"Get your hands off of me," she warned.

"Now, sugar, seeing as how you're going to be here awhile, we might as well be friendly." He squeezed, and Erin brought her knee up toward his crotch, but he blocked the move and twisted her arm around her back, hard enough that she let out a cry.

Mark launched himself at the thug, landing a knuckle-bruising blow that sent blood spurting from Tank's nose. Howling, the guard released Erin and swung the butt of his rifle against the side of Mark's head. Mark staggered back, his vision blurring. Erin's screams mingled with the pounding of his pulse and the animal growl that rose from Tank. Mark fell backward over one of the kitchen chairs and tried to regain his balance as Tank lunged toward him. He scanned the area for a weapon and grabbed for the chair, swinging it up to block a second blow from the rifle. Then the barrel of the weapon zeroed in on him, stalling his heart in his chest as he stared death in the face.

Chapter Five

"No!" Erin's scream tore through the noise of their struggle. "Don't be an idiot." She lunged toward the biggest thug, held back by the black guard, who wrapped his arms around her and lifted her off the ground as if she weighed no more than a pet dog. She kicked and flailed anyway, desperate to keep the other man from hurting Mark. "If you kill him before he finishes the bomb, Duane Braeswood will make sure you suffer," she shouted.

The big thug hesitated, and Mark staggered to his feet. He swayed, blood trailing down the side of his face, but he managed to glare at the guard, who snarled, but lowered the rifle. Then the thug turned and stalked to the door. The black guard shoved Erin toward Mark and seconds later the front door slammed behind them and the locks slid back into place.

"You're bleeding." She rushed to Mark, her fingers fluttering over the broken bruise on the side of his head, fearful of hurting him more if she touched him. But when he swayed alarmingly, she gripped him by the arm and led him to the bed. "Stay here and I'll get something to clean you up."

He opened his mouth as if to protest, then closed his eyes and said nothing. She hurried to the sink and ran cold water over a clean dishrag, keeping one eye on him in case he toppled over. The guard had hit him so hard she had been afraid at first that he'd been killed.

But he opened his eyes when she returned to his side, and sucked in his breath when she dabbed at the wound with the wet rag. "Sorry," she said, "but I need to clean up this blood. You've got a nasty bruise, and it broke the skin."

"At least I'm not dead," he said. "If you hadn't said that about Duane and the bomb, I probably would be."

"You shouldn't have punched him." Her hand tightened on his shoulder as she continued dabbing at the blood. Now that her initial terror had faded, she felt light-headed and shaky. "You didn't ask for me to come here and it's not your responsibility to defend me."

"I wasn't going to stand by and let him maul you." Mark turned his head to meet her gaze. "I didn't ask for you to come here, but I'm glad you're here."

The sad, defeated look had left his eyes, replaced with such strength and vitality she might have thought she was with a different man altogether. She lost track of everything in the heat of that gaze and for that split second, he wasn't hurt, she wasn't wearing a bomb around her neck, they weren't trapped and this whole nightmare had never happened. They were a man and a woman making a connection.

But under the circumstances, that kind of moment couldn't last. The situation was too dire, their need to get away too urgent. She squeezed his shoulder again, then dropped her hand. Her voice trembled only a little as she changed the subject. "Did you notice?" she asked. "The one who grabbed me after you hit the big guy left the door unguarded. We might be able to use that information."

"I don't think we can risk trying the same moves again." He touched the wound on the side of his head and winced. "Next time they might kill me. They might kill both of us."

"No, we can't risk it. But that tells us that

under the right circumstances, the man on the door will abandon his post." She stood. "Let's see what they brought us to eat."

The two plastic grocery bags the guard had carried in had tipped over and spilled their contents across the table: canned soup and fruit, sliced cheese and cheap lunch meat, a partially smashed loaf of bread, toaster pastries, instant coffee, crackers, corn chips, canned ravioli and a box of chocolate cupcakes. Mark picked up the cupcakes. "This is new," he said. "They never bring anything sweet."

Erin stared at the cupcakes, heart pounding. It was just a stupid box of cupcakes, but still…

"What's wrong?" Mark asked. "You look like you're going to faint." He put a steadying hand on her arm.

She shook her head, trying to clear the fog. "It's silly."

"But you think you know why the cupcakes are here this time?"

She swallowed, trying to keep her composure. "They're my favorite. When I was a kid, my mom would buy them as a special treat for my lunches. And even as an adult, she would keep them around for me." Erin swallowed tears at the memory of sitting at the kitchen table after school, peeling back the thick chocolate frosting with the white squiggle through the center to reveal the cream-filled chocolate cake beneath, while her mother sat across from her, sipping coffee and asking about her day. "Mom must have persuaded Duane to include them in the delivery for us. Either that, or it's his sick way of reminding me that he knows all about me." She turned away, fighting to regain control of her emotions.

Mark said nothing for a long moment, either because he didn't know what to say, or because he wanted to give her time to recover. When she turned to face him again, he had his hands in his pockets, his eyes fixed on her with a look of cautious sympathy. He cleared his throat. "If you're hungry, I can fix us some supper."

"Not yet. How are you feeling?"

"I've got a killer headache, but I'll live."

She leaned forward to look into his eyes, trying to remember the signs of a concussion from the first aid course she had taken prior to her first year of teaching. Something about uneven pupils—Mark's pupils looked okay. Maybe more than a little okay—dark and clear, set in the center of irises the color of a deep Alpine lake. They dilated a little now, and his breath caught, just as hers became more shallow. Her gaze shifted to his lips—well shaped and smooth, lips that looked as if they would know how to kiss a woman. She leaned toward him, wondering what he would think if she kissed him right now. Would he write it off as her reaction to the tension of the last hour? Could she blame their situation for the attraction she felt for him now?

He shifted and a bottle of mustard toppled and rolled toward the edge of the table. He deftly caught it and she used the moment to step back and collect herself. "I was checking to see if your pupils were the same size," she said. "If they're not, it's a sign of concussion."

"I guess I have a harder head than I thought."

The cupcake box pulled her thoughts back toward home. Suddenly, she wanted to talk about what had happened to her, as if talking would help make things more clear. "My mother was there—when I arrived at Duane's house," she said. "But she wasn't sick. If anything, she looked better than she had in years. She had gone along with the whole plan to lie and tell me she was dying. She said she thought it was the only way she would get to see me again. Duane told her he needed my help with a project and she believed him. She even told me it would be good for me to go with him, so I could see how important his work was."

"She probably doesn't know about the exact nature of the project," Mark said. "Maybe he even told her he was developing something beneficial."

Did he really believe that, or was he only trying to make her feel better? "There's no way she could not know about the people he's killed, the destruction he's caused," Erin said. "He doesn't try to keep it a secret. I heard him brag more than once about attacks he had masterminded."

"She couldn't know about that bomb he strapped on you," Mark said.

Erin touched the metal collar, her fingers ice-cold. "I hope she doesn't know." Her mind refused to accept that her mother would ever condone someone hurting her. "Duane would have hid that. At least, I hope he did."

"She obviously sees a different picture of Duane than we do," Mark said.

Erin sat and began lining up the canned goods in a row. "In her case, I guess love really is blind." But how could love—something that was supposed to be good—distort a person's vision so much?

Mark sat in the chair at the end of the table adjacent to her. "I think in the best relationships, each partner gives the other something they need. Maybe Duane gives your mom something she needs—security or devotion or something."

"What did your wife give you?" Erin asked. The better she got to know Mark, the more curious she was about the woman he mourned. "If it doesn't bother you too much to talk about her."

"When we met, she was a teaching assistant at the University of Colorado, where I was doing research. I spent most of my time in the lab, my head full of hypotheses and proofs, facts and figures. She was much more carefree and creative. Spontaneous and warm and so many things that I wasn't. Being with her made me feel anchored in the real world, the one outside my lab."

"And what do you think you gave her?"

His smile made Erin think he had been out of practice at forming the expression, as it came out more of a grimace. "I gave her a home and a child and security—all things she wanted but had never had. She lost both of her parents right out of high school and had been on her own ever since. I was a tenured professor with a good salary and a nice home in Boulder. I know that's what attracted her to me."

He made their relationship sound so…mercenary. "Are you saying you married for practical reasons?"

"Oh, I think Christy grew to truly love me. We didn't have a great, burning romance, but I never expected that. I was thirty-three when we met and pretty much married to my job. Having a wife and then a family made me happier than I would have thought possible. Christy got pregnant right away after we married and I thought my life was set."

Maybe the relationship he described wasn't so unusual. People came together for all sorts of reasons and formed a team that benefited them both. It was a simpler—and safer—plan than the kind of consuming love that had led her mother and other women like her to destroy their lives following a madman.

"So you were happy, then Duane came along and ruined everything," she said. "He specializes in that."

"I think he likes deciding the fates of others."

"Yes, he does." She rested her chin in her hands. "I'm always trying to figure out why people behave the way they do."

"It's the mathematician in you," he said. "Numbers obey logic, whereas people don't."

"I guess. Duane's parents died when he was very young, did you know that? I wonder sometimes if this is his way of maintaining control—or maybe exacting revenge on everyone who ever hurt him."

"Or maybe he's just nuts. People don't always act according to scientific principle."

She finished lining up the cans. "We'd better save most of this to take with us when we get out of here," she said. "We don't know how many days it will take us to reach help." She slid the cans of fruit, ravioli and soup over to one side. "I can stow them in a pillowcase."

"Better take a can opener and some utensils," he said. "There's matches on the shelf next to the sink."

"We'll need all our extra clothes and blankets," she said. "Do you have a coat?"

"I have an old ski jacket I was wearing when they snatched me. I'm more concerned about you. That denim jacket of yours isn't nearly warm enough for the kind of nighttime cold we're liable to experience in these mountains. It can get close to zero at these elevations this time of year."

"I can wear layers underneath it, and cut a hole in a blanket and wear it like a poncho," she said.

He nodded. "Moving around and keeping blood flowing to the hands and feet are most critical. We can't weigh ourselves down too heavily." He moved aside half the cans. "Our best bet will be to cover as much ground as possible, as quickly as possible. Stay off the roads, but parallel them when we can. Navigate using landmarks so we don't travel in circles. Try to avoid cliffs, box canyons and other choke points where we would have to backtrack."

She stared at him. "How does a man who spent most of his time in a lab know so much about backcountry travel?"

"I never said I spent all my time in the lab. I hiked a lot, too. Solo trips into the backcountry, mostly. I was on a trip like that when Duane's men kidnapped me and brought me here."

"They ambushed you in the middle of no-where?"

"They were waiting at the trailhead when my brother dropped me off. After he left, they followed me up the trail and attacked me. They knocked me out and when I awoke I was tied up in a cave somewhere in the mountains."

"No offense, but why go to so much trouble to get you?" she asked. "There must be a lot of scientists who do what you do, including some who would buy in to Duane's crazy plan to re-form the government by destroying it."

Mark rubbed his hand over his eyes. "I've thought about that a lot. I think it's because I wrote an article on the future of nuclear technology for a popular magazine. It got a lot of buzz on the internet. In the article I noted that nuclear weapons had shrunk in size over the years and that some people thought a so-called suitcase nuke was within reach. I was much more interested in the technical possibilities for nuclear power generation, but Duane and people of his ilk latched on to the few comments I made about weapons. Duane decided I must know more than I'd let on in my paper. Apparently, once he gets an idea in his head, he refuses to let it go."

"Yes, he is obsessive," she said. "I heard rumors about other people he kidnapped because he decided they—or their loved ones—could be useful to him."

"How are you useful to him?" Mark asked.

"I'm not. I don't know why he brought me here, except that he hates the way I've always defied him and this is his way of punishing me." She put a hand to the collar.

"I think you're here to influence me," Mark said.

"How can I influence you? We're strangers."

"You're a beautiful young woman. If I don't

give Duane what he wants by the deadline he set, you die. No decent human being could be unaffected by that kind of threat."

"I'm not convinced everyone would be so motivated by the threat of a stranger's death."

"Except you're not a stranger to me now. We've made a connection. You're the person who made me feel alive—feel human again—after so many months of isolation."

She looked away. What could she say to that? Except that she felt a connection to him, as well. In some ways, they were very much alike. While he'd been forced to live alone in this remote mountain hideaway, she had kept herself apart from the people around her, afraid her connection with Duane Braeswood might lead to them being harmed.

But she didn't have to protect Mark from that part of her life. In a little over twenty-four hours, he had forced her to lower a barrier she hadn't even realized she had built around herself.

"The only thing that kept me going before now was the thought of keeping my daughter safe," he said. "Maybe they sensed that motivation was weakening the longer I went with no word from her. I don't even know for sure if she's all right."

Erin took his hand, needing the contact as much for herself as to comfort him. "When we get out of here you can find her again. Your brother and the FBI will bring down Duane and you won't have to worry anymore."

He squeezed her hand, holding on tightly. "That's the new goal. We just have to figure out how to make it happen."

"The next time they bring food," she said, "we'll be ready with the acid."

"It may be a while. In the past when they were angry with me about something, they let me go hungry for a few days as punishment."

"There's a special place in hell for people like them." She reluctantly released his hand and stood. "We might as well eat what they brought."

They settled on a dinner of canned ravioli and applesauce, and ate in silence. As Mark cleared the table she said, her voice low, "When we were talking earlier, I forgot all about the possibility that the guards might be listening to us. Do you really think they have this place bugged?"

He piled their dishes in the sink and ran water over them. "I don't know. I was probably being a little paranoid—a side effect of what has essentially been solitary confinement for over a year. After all, since I've been here by myself, what would they hear? I don't think we really have anything to worry about."

She stood and stretched. "What is it about doing nothing all day that's so exhausting?" she asked, and stifled a yawn.

"The tension gets to you. That, and the fact that there's nothing else to do after dark but sleep. Most days I spend an hour or two working out. It fills the time and I tell myself it's good to keep in shape."

She remembered the feel of his body against hers. He had definitely kept in shape. She glanced toward the bed, and the memory of waking in his arms this morning was so real she could almost feel the warmth of his fingers. "Speaking of sleeping—my offer still stands to bed down on the floor."

He shut off the water and began sponging plates. "That isn't necessary. We can share the bed again. You don't have anything to fear from me."

She wasn't worried about him—not really. But her own strong attraction to him unsettled her. She couldn't say what she might do if he wrapped his arms around her in the darkness again.

Maybe he mistook her silence for disagreement. He dried his hands and turned to face her. "Look, we're both adults," he said. "I don't know about your past relationships, but it's been a long time since I slept with a woman. You're beautiful and I like you and yes, I'm attracted to you. But I'm not going to do anything you don't want."

The look in his eyes sent heat curling through her and she struggled to keep her voice even. "I haven't been involved with anyone in a long time," she said. "And yes, I am attracted to you, too. But I don't think, under the circumstances, that acting on that attraction would be a good idea."

"No, it wouldn't." He crossed his arms over his chest. He had rolled up the sleeves of his shirt and the corded muscles of his forearms stood out. "So are you okay with sharing a bed?"

"Sure." Though she doubted she would get much sleep with him so near.

She helped him finish the dishes, the light outside fading away as they did so. He lit the oil lamp in the center of the table and left the box of matches beside it, then gestured toward the bathroom. "You can go first."

She debated taking a shower, but no telling what water would do to the collar, so she settled for a sponge bath, then brushed her teeth and resigned herself to sleeping in her clothes for a second night. Mark was waiting when she emerged from the bathroom, and slipped in behind her. She removed her shoes and slid under the covers and lay staring at the ceiling until he returned. He blew out the lamp and slid under the blanket beside her.

Though their bodies didn't touch, the heat of him seeped into her, and the subtle scent of him surrounded her—a mixture of shaving cream and lab reagents and male that left her longing to inch toward him. She shifted, trying—and failing—to get comfortable.

"I know it's hard, but try to sleep," he said. "Everything is that much more difficult if you're exhausted."

"They don't ever come in here at night, do they? The guards?" The thought of one of those creeps watching her while she slept made her skin crawl.

"They haven't before. I'm a pretty light sleeper, so I think I'd know."

"Yeah, but I wasn't here before," she said.

"Good point." He slid his arm around her. "I won't let them do anything to you. I promise."

She let herself relax against him. After a moment she moved closer and rested her head on his shoulder. "Is this all right?"

His arm tightened around her. "It's more than all right. Now try to get some sleep."

She felt safe in Mark's arms—safe enough to drift into the most restful sleep she had had in weeks. She was deep in slumber, surrounded by darkness and the warmth and strength of Mark's body against hers, when the blare of a light and a man's shout roused her.

"Get up!" someone ordered.

She shielded her eyes with her hand and tried to see who was speaking. "What?"

"Mr. Braeswood has ordered you moved," the intruder said. "Now get going."

Chapter Six

Heart slamming against her chest, Erin gaped at the three men with guns who had burst into the cabin. An icy breeze swept through the open door behind them, fluttering papers on the workbench and raising goose bumps on her bare arms.

"What are you talking about?" Mark's voice was sharp, and much more alert than she felt.

"You're moving." The beefy guy who had fought with Mark earlier prodded him with the butt of the rifle. "Get up and get dressed to go."

Erin scrambled from the bed before the guard could focus on her, and began pulling on clothes, layering a sweater and her jacket over the T-shirt and jeans she had worn to bed, then shoving her feet into her boots.

Mark dressed, too, also pulling on his coat. The blond guard and the wiry black man who had accompanied him earlier kept watch over them while a third guard lit an oil lamp and began packing the items on the workbench into a cardboard box that had once held vodka. The lamplight reflected off the blond peach fuzz of this younger guard, whose acne-scarred face made him look as if he was scarcely out of his teens.

As Erin came more awake, her fear increased. If she and Mark were being moved, maybe it was to a more secure location. They might be separated. Or maybe Duane's men planned to take them out into the wilderness and shoot them. She had heard rumors once that this was the way he had dealt with one of his followers who had done something to displease him. She caught Mark's eye, trying to telegraph her panic.

His gaze locked to hers and he gave an almost imperceptible nod. A clatter from the workbench made him jerk his head in that direction. "Hey!" His shout made her jump. "What do you think you're doing?"

Before either guard could react, Mark had crossed the room and grabbed the arm of the man who was packing up the lab supplies. "This equipment is delicate and in some cases dangerous," he snapped. "Break anything and you jeopardize everything I've been working on—everything Mr. Braeswood ordered me to do." He yanked the box from the man's hands. "Let me take care of this. You and one of the other men see to that trunk." He indicated the silver metal trunk beneath the bench. "Don't jostle it, and whatever you do, don't drop it. It's the key element in this entire project."

Erin stared at the box, a chill shuddering through her. She hadn't noticed it before. Was it really that dangerous?

The guard stepped back and eyed the trunk warily. "What's in it?" he asked.

Mark focused on rearranging items in the box. "Do you know why I'm here?" he asked.

The guard furrowed his brow. "You're building some sort of secret weapon?"

"A nuclear bomb." He turned to face the guard, one hand on the box beside him. He nodded to the trunk. "I'm almost finished. I won't be to blame if you screw this up."

"Quit wasting time and get moving," the blond guard, who had moved closer to Erin, said.

The young man with Mark shrugged, slung his rifle across his back and bent to pick up the trunk. He grunted and managed to lift it a few inches.

"Get someone to help you!" Mark's voice was sharp with annoyance. "Didn't you hear anything I just said?"

The door was still open, letting in a bitter cold. Erin grabbed the blanket from the bed and wrapped it around her shoulders, though some of the chill that engulfed her came from inside her. What had happened to the calm, stoic man she had come to know? This version of Mark was a crazed mad scientist, exactly the kind of man who would build a nuclear weapon for a maniac. And what was really in that trunk? Had he actually been building Duane's bomb, despite his denials to her?

"Trey, you help move the box." The blond guard indicated the black man, who had positioned himself by the door. "Don't waste any more time."

Trey moved forward to help the younger man with the trunk. The two of them hefted it and shuffled toward the exit. Mark began packing more items from the workbench into the box and the blond guard positioned himself between the two prisoners, his rifle cradled in his arms.

Time, which had been moving forward too quickly up to this point, seemed to slow down as the men with the trunk stepped through the door and onto the porch. The thud of their booted feet on the wooden steps echoed in the middle-of-the-night stillness. The lamp sputtered and Erin pulled the blanket more tightly around her. Mark stood beside the laboratory bench, his hand wrapped around a tall glass beaker. The blond man took a step toward the bench, blocking Erin's view of Mark. She glanced back toward the open door.

"Run!" The command had her moving toward the door before the meaning of the word had fully registered. The blond screamed, an animal howl of rage, and she turned to see him with his hands over his eyes, liquid dripping down his face, the rifle on the floor, almost at her feet. He shouted curses as Mark hurled a now-empty glass beaker at him, then grabbed Erin's hand and dragged her toward the door. She pulled away and scooped up the rifle, then raced with him out onto the front porch.

MARK PAUSED AT the top of the steps, trying to get his bearings. In front of him and a little to the left, light spilled from the open back hatch of a black Humvee, where the other two guards struggled to shove the heavy trunk inside. One of them looked up and shouted, jolting Mark into action once more. Pulling Erin along behind him, he raced past the vehicle and down the rutted track that led away from the cabin.

The thunder of gunfire shattered the night stillness, and shards of rock pelted the legs of his hiking pants. Erin screamed, and he held on to her more tightly. They stumbled along in the dim light of a quarter moon. Bright white patches glowed amid the rocks and he realized with a start that it had snowed recently.

The rev of an engine behind them told him the guards had started the Hummer. "We can't outrun a vehicle," Erin sobbed.

"No. But a vehicle—even a Hummer—can't drive cross-country here." He yanked her off the road and they stumbled and slid down a slope of loose rock. They wove in and out among stunted piñon and junipers, and clusters of boulders like crouching giants silvered in the moonlight.

"I have to stop." Erin pulled him back against one of these boulder formations, her breath coming in ragged gasps.

"Are you okay?" He moved closer to study her face in the moonlight. Her hair was a wild tumble around her face, and the blanket flapped behind her like a cape.

She nodded and swallowed. "Just winded. And scared. What about you?"

"The same." He took a deep breath. "I kept expecting a bullet to slam into my back at any minute."

She clutched his shoulder, fingers digging in hard. "What was that all about back there?" she asked. "All that rage over the lab equipment and the trunk?"

"I wanted to catch them off guard. I've been so passive these past few months, that's what they expect from me. I thought if I stunned them enough, they would agree to do as I asked. After all, they're men who are used to obeying commands."

"You certainly startled me." She still looked wary. "What was really in that trunk?"

"Exactly what I told them—a nuclear bomb. Or rather, something that looks like a nuclear bomb, minus the fuel or the means of detonation. I built it months ago as a decoy, in case Duane ever pressed me for results. I figured I could show him the trunk and he would believe I had been making a good-faith effort. It's not the suitcase nuke he wanted, but any serious reading on the subject would tell him he was asking the impossible. I wanted to placate him with something that at least looked probable, even if it wasn't the real thing."

"Why would you try to placate someone like him?" she asked, with surprising vehemence.

"Because I would do anything to get away from him and get back to my daughter, or at least to keep him away from her, including acting as if I was as dedicated to his crackpot cause as he is."

Her shoulders sagged. "I'm sorry," she whispered. "I'm so angry at Duane I forget that I'm not the only one he's hurt."

"I don't blame you for being suspicious," Mark said. "After all, you don't really know me."

"No. But I want to trust you. I want to believe you're a man who can be trusted."

Before he could respond to this confession, or even process it, she pushed away from the rock. "We should be going," she said. "They'll be coming after us."

He glanced over his shoulder, but heard no sounds of pursuit. Maybe the guards were being stealthy, but he didn't think they would be at that point yet. "It will be morning before they can see well enough to track us," he said. "We need to use that time to get as far away from the cabin as possible."

"I don't know if I can keep up," she said. "I can't see where I'm going and I keep stumbling on the rock. Maybe we should split up so I won't slow you down."

"No way," he said. "If not for you, I wouldn't have worked up the nerve to try to get away." He squeezed her arm. "You're doing great. Bringing that blanket was a good idea." They would need all the warmth they could get. Already his fingers were numb and aching.

"I got something better than a blanket," she said.

When she pulled the rifle from beneath the blanket, he could have kissed her.

And then he was kissing her, anxiety and relief and pent-up need driving him to pull her tightly against him and press his lips to hers. She shivered slightly and he stilled, unwilling to move away, but knowing he would if she protested or pushed at him.

Then all the stiffness went out of her and she melted against him, her arms sliding beneath his coat and encircling him, her mouth slanting against his, lips parting slightly so that he tasted her heady sweetness.

He had forgotten how wonderful a woman could feel, how soft and strong, delicate yet powerful, every feminine part of her designed to remind him of what it meant to be a man. She shaped her body to his, and he slid his thigh between hers, her sigh of delight warming him as no fire could.

He slid his hand to her side and knocked the rifle that hung from her shoulder, startling them both. Looking flustered, she jerked away. "I... I didn't mean for that to happen," she stammered. "I just..."

"It's okay." He busied himself zipping up the ski jacket, as if he could somehow keep in the memory of her hands on him. "It happened. It's okay." More than okay.

"We'd better get going," she said. She looked to her left and right—anywhere but at him. "Which way?"

He started to apologize, but he wasn't sorry about the kiss. For now, he'd follow her lead in pretending it had never happened. "We can try to parallel the road as much as possible, but that may not be feasible all the time," he said. He glanced overhead. "How much do you know about navigating by the stars?"

"About as much as I know about nuclear physics," she said. "What about you?"

"Nothing," he admitted.

"I was hoping it was a secret hobby of yours," she said. "Along with gourmet cooking with wild foods and erecting palatial wilderness shelters."

"Sorry to disappoint." He smiled, even though he doubted she could see much of his expression in the dark. He felt so much lighter and freer out here in the open, even though they were far from out of danger. He put his hand on the rifle. "Let me carry this."

She relinquished the weapon. "Do you know how to use it?" she asked.

"I do." And he would, if necessary. He took her hand. "We'll stick close to the road for now," he said. "We should be able to hear anyone coming."

Even walking in the roadway, the going was tough. The twin ruts in the snow were barely visible in the pale moonlight, strewn with loose rock in others. The cold was numbing, slicing through his clothes as if they were made of paper. Even with the blanket wrapped over her thin jacket, Erin must be freezing. They picked their way across an icy stream, then fought to keep their balance on a steep pitch. "I wish I had grabbed a flashlight, too," she said.

"It would be too risky to use it," he said. "I did palm the box of matches while I was pretending to pack the items from the workbench. They're in my pocket, but we ought to save them for starting a fire when we get somewhere safe to do so."

"You sound so confident," she said. "I'm completely out of my element here."

"In the morning we should be able to get our bearings and come up with a plan," he said. "All we have to do until then is focus on staying alive."

"Hiding from crazed killers, not freezing to death and not falling off a cliff. Piece of cake."

"Well, when you put it that—" He broke off the words, tensed. "Did you hear that?"

They listened to the distant growl that grew louder. "It's a vehicle," she said. "Headed this way."

The roar grew much louder as the bright, blue-white beams of headlights swept around the corner. Mark pulled her to the side of the road, where they crouched behind a rock outcropping, out of range, for the moment, of those searching beams. "We've got to get out of here," she said, her voice trembling.

He stared toward the approaching headlights. Behind them, a third beam swept the sides of the road—probably a handheld spotlight. In daylight, he might have a chance of taking out the driver, and maybe one of the other men, but he would never be able to shoot three of them before one disabled him, and probably Erin, as well. With the bright lights blinding him, he didn't have a chance.

"This way," he said, He pulled her around the outcropping of rock, feeling his way along a narrow ledge. By the time the vehicle crawled past them, they were well behind the screen of rock.

Erin sagged against him as the sound of the engine faded. "Thank God. I was sure they were going to see us."

"They didn't see us." Not this time. They still had an hour or more before daylight to make their way down this mountain toward safety. It wouldn't be easy, but maybe they were past the worst of it now.

Then the ground gave way beneath them and they were sliding and falling, careening down a steep slope, Erin's scream echoing in his ear as she was torn from his grasp.

Chapter Seven

Erin clawed at the ground as she slid over it, rocks and chunks of ice tearing at her skin and catching at her clothes. She bounced and skidded down the slope, grappling for purchase and finding none. She felt, rather than saw, Mark hurtle past her, and realized she was screaming, her throat raw, the sound echoing off the rocks around them.

Then, as suddenly as she had started moving, she stopped, something bulky and soft cushioning the blow of her landing. Somehow, she had landed on Mark. He wrapped his arms around her. "Are you okay?" he asked.

Hearing his voice, knowing he was all right, made her all but sob with relief. "I think so. You?"

"A lot of bruises, but I'm okay." He sat up, bringing her with him. "I still have the rifle."

"I lost the blanket," she said. She peered up the slope, but could make out nothing but lighter and darker gray smudges of rock. "What happened?"

"I think the ledge gave way. We're lucky we didn't fall farther." He stood and helped her to her feet. They had come to rest in a dry wash, choked with rock and shrubby trees. The air smelled of fresh pine and damp earth. Though the sky was beginning to lighten, she could no longer see the road from here. The knowledge of how close they had come to death shook her. "We could have been killed," she said. She touched the collar at her neck — it could have gone off. She swayed, unsteady at the thought.

"We weren't." His voice was strong. "We just have to stay alert. We won't take unnecessary chances, but we won't be so cautious we miss our best opportunity to get out of here."

"Do you think the guards heard us?" she asked.

He glanced overhead, back the way they had come. "I think if they had, we'd know it by now. The snow swallows up a lot of sound. For now, we had better stay put until daylight, when we can see where we're going. We need to get back up to the road and we can't do that in the dark."

She hugged her arms across her chest and shifted from foot to foot. "It feels colder down here. Maybe I'm in shock." Her feet ached with cold, and her fingers and face were numb.

"Canyons like this trap the cold." He picked up a branch that had probably been broken in their fall. "Let's build a fire. That will warm us up."

"Do you think that's safe?"

"We can shelter it under the overhang of the cliff, where it will be harder to see from above. As long as we keep the blaze small, it should be all right. We need to warm up before we go on."

"Good idea." She moved alongside him, gathering kindling.

"Are you feeling okay?" he asked. "No dizziness or unsteadiness?"

"I'm okay." She picked up a large pinecone. "Maybe I just needed to move around." She would take his advice and not think about what had almost happened, and focus instead on what she wished would happen. She would envision warm rooms, hot food and people around her who weren't trying to kill her.

When they had gathered a double armload of kindling and larger pieces of wood, he cleared a space on the frozen ground and set about building a fire. He worked quickly, his hands deftly arranging the smaller sticks and larger pieces of wood. He lit a match and touched it to the mixture of pine needles and pocket lint he had piled beneath a pyramid of twigs. The flame caught and spread, licking at the sticks until they, too, were ablaze.

"You look like you've done this before," she said, moving to stand closer to the warmth, and thus to him.

"I always did my best thinking in the wilderness."

"What are your best thoughts now?"

He didn't answer right away, the snap of the fire the only sound. "I'm thinking that I'm glad I'm not doing this alone," he said after a moment.

The desolation in his voice pinched at her. She had endured only a few weeks of deprivation thanks to Duane. Mark had been the madman's pawn for fourteen months. "You've been alone too much lately," she said.

He sat back on his heels and stared into the fire, the shadows of the flames flickering across the planes and hollows of his face. It wasn't a classically handsome face, but his strong jaw and high forehead hinted at his strength and intelligence. "I'm not someone who tolerates the company of others well," he said. "Though I make exceptions for people I care about."

Was he saying he cared about her? She pushed the thought away. "Why do you think they decided to move us?"

"I want to hear your theory before I share mine."

"I wondered if they heard us talking about our plans to get away and decided to preempt them."

He nodded. "That's what I wondered, too. But it could have just as easily been part of Duane's original plan, to keep us off guard."

"Do you think they're still looking for us?" she asked. "I mean, maybe now that they have that trunk and what they think is a bomb, Duane will be happy and let us go."

"A man who will go to the kind of trouble and expense he has in order to carry out a plan he's concocted isn't going to just drop things," Mark said. "And he doesn't let people get away with crossing him, either."

"No." She ran a finger under the edge of the collar. "No, he doesn't." She was a prime example of what happened to people who crossed Duane. He never simply forgot about them and let them go. She lowered herself to the ground beside the fire. As her body thawed, her mind became less numb, too. "Can they do anything with the contents of that trunk?" she asked. "I mean, could they find another scientist or explosives expert to build them a real nuclear bomb?" Knowing the trunk even existed had come as a shock to her.

Mark sat on the ground beside her, and fed a larger stick to the blaze. "It's doubtful. Given more time and money and higher grade ore, it might happen, but Duane strikes me as a man who's running out of patience."

"I think you're right, and that worries me. He has a lot of resources, and from what I've seen, he doesn't mind throwing lots of money and man power at whatever goal he's after. What if he brings in dogs to track us? Or follows us with a helicopter?"

"He might do those things, but the fall could work in our favor. The searchers won't expect to find us down here. That could throw them off the track. We need to take advantage of whatever lead we've gained."

"It would help if we had the slightest idea where we are." She craned her head to scan the embankment they had slid down. Boulders the size of furniture and logs scattered like straw pocked the landscape.

"I'm pretty sure this drainage runs north-south." He pointed to the heavy growth of moss on the side of a tree near them. "Moss like this tends to grow on the north side of trees. The road ran that direction, too, so I think we're paralleling the road, but about fifty feet lower."

"So we keep following this and we'll get to wherever the road leads?" she asked.

"Maybe. Or we could end up in a box canyon that goes nowhere." He joined her in looking up the slope. "As I said before, I think we're going to have to climb back up there."

She swallowed. "And to think I left my mountain-climbing gear at home."

He caught her gaze and held it. "I'm glad you still have your sense of humor. Things could get pretty tough before we get out of here. But we're going to be tougher."

Right. Except that with him she felt more vulnerable than she had in years—since before Duane had come into her life and distorted everything she knew about love and trust. "Do you know what frightens me the most?" she asked.

"No, but I'm willing to listen if you want to tell me."

She stared into the coals that glowed orange

amid the remnants of branches white with ash. "I'm terrified that I missed my chance to stop him," she said. "When I first left home I didn't tell anyone the things I knew—and the things I suspected—about Duane's activities, because I worried about what it would do to my mother. I thought if I kept quiet, she would be all right and I could forget all about him. When she came to live with me I suggested we go to the authorities, but the idea upset her so much I didn't pursue it. These last few weeks with him and his men—learning the extent of his madness and the lengths he will go to in order to carry out his twisted plans—I realize how much my silence has cost. What if he finds someone to arm that bomb and he kills hundreds, even thousands, of innocent people? How can I live with the knowledge that I could have stopped him, but when I had the chance I chose to do nothing?"

"You were afraid for yourself, but even more frightened for your mother," Mark said. "Believe me, I know how paralyzing that kind of fear can be. It's the same fear that kept me working in that cabin for months. Duane bought my silence with his threats to my daughter, but in the end the cost was much greater. I lost my perspective and I almost lost my will to go on. You've given that back to me. Now I realize the only way I can protect Mandy is to fight back against the vision of the world that Duane wants to make a reality." He reached over and took her hand. "It helps me to know I'm not fighting alone. And I think we have an advantage over Duane."

"We're not insane. I suppose that helps."

A ghost of a smile flitted through his eyes before he sobered once more. "He thinks we're both passive, cowed by what he's done to us. He's guilty of one of the primary errors in scientific research—making a false assumption. He's expecting one result—for us to fail—and has an unconscious bias to pay more attention to any evidence that supports his assumption. We can take advantage of that and attack him when he's not expecting it."

Everything Mark said made perfect sense, and Erin found herself believing he might be right. But the reality of their situation— stranded in the middle of nowhere in bitter cold, with a bomb strapped around her neck— made it more difficult to visualize the success he seemed so sure was theirs. She took a deep breath. "I guess the first thing we need to do is get out of this ravine."

"Right." He glanced at the sky. Though

low clouds obscured the sun, it was now light enough to see clearly. He stood and began to kick dirt onto the fire. "It won't be the easiest climb, but it's doable. We'll take it slow and choose the route carefully. You go first and I'll be right behind to catch you if you start to fall."

She helped him put out the fire and scatter the ashes, even as she mourned the loss of warmth. As they worked, the cold was already seeping through her clothes, making her teeth chatter. They swept branches over the area and scattered gravel, trying to obscure any obvious signs that they had stopped here. Then Mark turned to survey the slope they had to climb. "It's a little less steep there, where that gravel has washed down." He traced a line in the air and she followed the direction he was pointing. "Those trees and bushes will give us hand-and footholds," he said. "And the overhang, just to the right, gives us some cover while we check things out up top."

"Right. Piece of cake." She rubbed her hands together. "You go that way and I'll find the elevator."

He chuckled and put a hand at her back. She liked the way it felt, his palm pressed to her spine, providing both guidance and reassurance. They stopped at the bottom of the area he had indicated, which didn't look any less steep to her. "Grab hold of that branch and put your foot on that tree root, then pull yourself up," he instructed.

Proceeding this way, with him directing her from behind, the climb wasn't so bad. She managed to push away the image of her falling and sending them both crashing back down, and focused on carefully placing each foot and using her hands to haul herself up. Before she had traveled too many feet she was panting and beginning to sweat, her earlier chill forgotten.

The trouble began about halfway up, when a narrow stream of cold water, perhaps from some underground spring, trickled down the bank, turning the soil in the area to slick mud. When Erin tried to plant her foot, it skidded from under her, and only her death grip on a spindly scrub oak kept her from hurtling back down the slope.

Mark was at her back once more. "Try digging your toe in and kicking in a step," he said.

She did as he suggested and after three hard kicks was rewarded with a firmer foothold. She proceeded this way up the rest of the slope, until she came to rest under the sheltering overhang of a rock outcropping. She was winded, her hands aching from gripping the cold, slippery branches and rocks that had served as hand-and footholds. Her hands, face and clothing were streaked with a reddish mud that smelled slightly metallic and felt gritty against her skin.

Mark joined her beneath the rock overhang after a few minutes. He looked as disheveled and dirty as she felt, but a grin split his face. "I haven't climbed like that in months," he said. "It felt good."

She couldn't help but return the smile. "It does feel good." She'd won a battle of sorts— against the steep slope and against her own fears. "What next?"

"Let's wait here a bit and catch our breath and see if we hear anything alarming up there."

But the only sounds to break the early morning stillness were the deep intake and exhalation of their own breaths, the trickle from the dripping spring, and the lonesome call of a dove.

"I think we're okay." Mark spoke in a whisper, his mouth close to her ear, his warm breath tickling her neck above the metal collar, sending a startling current of heat through her. "I'll go first, then I can pull you up," he said, shifting to move past her.

A tremble shot through her when his body

brushed hers. She told herself it was simply the aftereffect of adrenaline from the climb, but the word *liar* came quickly on the heels of that thought. This strong, virile version of a man she was already attracted to stirred a more primitive desire deep within her. Mark Renfro might be an overly serious scientist, but right now he was a very sexy scientist.

She pressed her body against the cool earth and listened to the scrape of rock against his boots and the soft grunts of exertion he made as he swung onto the ledge from which they had fallen earlier. She didn't even realize she had been holding her breath until she heard his voice again and saw his hand reaching down for her. "All clear," he said. "Hold on tight and I'll pull you up."

Half climbing, half letting him lift her, she struggled onto the ledge and lay for a moment in the dirt, panting. He helped her to her feet and led the way along a narrow path that must have been made by animals. From time to time she caught a glimpse of the road, but the landscape around them remained silent. Maybe Duane's men had temporarily abandoned the search and were awaiting further instructions from their boss. Or maybe they had headed off in another direction.

All we need is a little more time, she thought. *As soon as we get to a phone, we'll be all right.*

They walked for the better part of an hour without speaking. The sun disappeared completely behind a bank of heavy clouds and the wind picked up, cutting through Erin's jacket and jeans. She hugged her arms across her chest and bowed against the wind, gritting her teeth to keep them from chattering. She ached with the cold, and stumbled once, almost colliding with Mark, who marched stoically along in front of her. He had to be almost as chilled as she was, but he showed no signs of it, walking confidently upright, the rifle slung across his chest. Knowing he was watching for any sign of trouble, she was able to relax a little. *Think warm thoughts*, she told herself. *Hot chocolate. Mulled wine. Chicken soup. Roaring fires and warm quilts. Naked bodies twined together beneath those quilts, in front of that fire...*

A shout broke the stillness—a man's voice, risen in alarm. Mark dived to the side of the trail, pulling her with him, even as gunfire raked the area where they had just stood. She pressed against him, trying to make herself as small as possible. "How did they find us so soon?" she whispered.

He shook his head, his hands gripping her

shoulders, holding her tightly to him. "I don't know, but they aren't that close. The shots came from somewhere on the ridge to our left. He must have spotted us and fired from there."

"If you're trying to reassure me, it's not working. With that rifle, he doesn't have to be close in order to kill us."

"Point taken. But if we can keep from getting shot, we have a better chance of evading them at this distance. It will take them a while to get to this trail. By the time they do, we'll be gone."

"But he has us pinned down."

"Not necessarily. He may not have seen where we ended up."

"Don't make assumptions, Professor."

"Then let's perform a little experiment." Before she could object, he picked up a rock about the size of his fist, wound up and fired it out of their hiding place. It landed with a clatter fifty feet up the trail and bounced twice before coming to rest at the base of a tree. A split second later bullets thudded into the tree, sending splinters flying. Mark grinned.

"What are you so happy about?" she asked.

"He didn't fire at us. He didn't see where the rock came from. He was only reacting to the movement and sound. We can use that to our advantage."

"How?"

"We'll head that way." He pointed down the trail, back toward the cabin. "If we move slowly and keep to the cover of the trees, he shouldn't see us."

"But it's the wrong direction," she said.

"When they give up and start moving in another direction we can backtrack," he said. "Right now it's more important to get away from them than to stick to our goal."

He was right, of course, but that didn't make this knowledge any easier to accept. At this rate she'd be frozen or crippled by the time they reached safety. Better to swallow the bitter medicine and get on with it. "I'll follow you," she said.

He slipped through the narrow line of trees and shrubs between the road and their trail with the stealth of a cat burglar. She followed, trying to place her steps where he had placed his, trusting that his instincts were better than hers when it came to moving through the wilderness. She collided with his back when he stopped suddenly, frozen like a deer in the headlights. "What is it?" she whispered. "What's wrong?"

"This is where we fell before," he said. "The whole ledge collapsed, remember? There's no way to cross."

The feeling of falling was fresh enough to make her heart pound. She turned away. "Then we have to go back," she said. Not waiting for him to answer, she moved forward, her steps more sure now, covering familiar territory. Whoever had been shooting at them up on the ridge had held his fire for several minutes now. She prayed he wasn't training a pair of binoculars—or a rifle scope—on them right this minute, preparing to fire the bullet that would end this whole crazy game Duane had forced them to play.

Mark caught up with her. "Let me go first," he said.

"No, I've got this." She walked faster. Relying on Mark to always take the lead had been a mistake. She had to force herself past this paralyzing fear.

The first shots exploded above and behind them. Erin couldn't hold back her scream, and terror propelled her forward. She ran blindly, branches lashing her face and arms, feet slipping on loose rock. She didn't know if Mark followed, or even if their unseen pursuers fired more shots. Fear made her blind and deaf to anything but her own pounding heart and her need to get away.

She had no idea how long she had been running when she tripped and landed hard on her knees, rocks tearing her jeans and bloodying her hands. Sobbing, she slumped in the dirt, braced for the bullets she was sure would come.

Instead, strong arms embraced her, then lifted her and carried her deeper into the undergrowth. "Shh. It's okay. You're going to be okay." He repeated the words over and over, a soothing mantra that eventually slowed her heart and beat back the wave of terror that had crowded out reason. When she was finally able to open her eyes and lift her head from his shoulder, she stared into eyes dark with concern. "What happened?" she asked.

"You panicked. It could have happened to anyone."

She sniffed. "I know I panicked. I mean, what happened to the man who was shooting at us?"

Mark shook his head. "I don't know. Maybe you outran his field of vision. Or he was too far away to clearly see what was happening. Or your guardian angel is working overtime."

"I'm sorry." She tried to pull away, but he

held her gently but firmly to him. "My stupidity could have killed us both."

"You weren't stupid," he said. "You were scared. I know the difference."

"I don't know what came over me." She forced herself to meet his gaze. "You should have run while you had the chance."

"I'm not going to leave you." He shook her gently. "I know a little bit about post-traumatic stress," he said. "I think that's what you're suffering from."

"What are you talking about? I never fought in a war."

"But you did. You've been at war for years with Duane and your own conscience. That's bound to take a toll."

She rested her forehead against Mark's and closed her eyes once more. "I'm just so tired of being afraid all the time."

"I understand. I really do."

She believed he did. He had endured his own hell of wondering and waiting for the other shoe to drop, not knowing when Duane would tire of his games and decide to kill him, or his daughter. Of all the people in this world, Mark knew a little of what she had been through. For whatever reason, his newfound freedom had given him courage, while hers had allowed all the feelings she had been avoiding for too long to overwhelm her. But knowing he understood gave her strength, too.

"Maybe the worst is over," she said.

"Even if it's not, we'll get through this," he said. "Together."

As her shaking subsided and the panic receded, a new wave of unsettling sensations stole over her. Heat from his body warmed her. The brush of his muscular arm sent a tremor through her. The desire to be away from this place and this situation faded, replaced by a different longing that was just as fierce—to be even closer to him. His arms tightened around her and she met his gaze once more. Her heart felt too big for her chest as she recognized the same wanting in his eyes.

His gaze shifted to her mouth, and she lifted her chin, angling toward him. If he didn't kiss her right now she wouldn't be able to stand it. She slid one hand up to cup the back of his head, threading her fingers into his thick dark hair and urging him toward her.

He let out a sound that was half sigh, half groan, and covered her lips with his. The last bit of frost melted from her bones as he skillfully teased her mouth, the silk of his tongue and the roughness of his beard setting every nerve ending humming. She trailed her hand along his jaw, reveling in the masculine feel of his unshaved face. How had she ever mistaken him for a passive, even weak, academic? The man in the lab coat had merely been a disguise for his true role of rugged outdoorsman.

They broke apart at last, both panting and dazed. "Lousy timing for this," he said, his voice rough. He glanced at the woods around them and the reality of the situation crashed over her once more. She moved out of his embrace and wrapped her arms around herself, though his warmth still enveloped her. "Yeah. Lousy timing." Running from killers wasn't the best time to give in to her attraction to this man. How much of her feelings were due to fear, and how much were genuine?

"You look cold," he said. "Why don't we build another fire and try to get warm?"

"The smoke could attract the wrong kind of attention," she said.

"We won't stay long," he said. "Just long enough to thaw the worst of the chill." He flexed his fingers. "I can't feel my hands anymore."

The prospect of warmth won out over her fear of discovery. "All right. A fire would be good."

He patted her shoulder. "You find some kindling and I'll get some bigger wood."

Keeping Mark within sight, she searched the ground for the dried twigs and pinecones they had used to build their fire earlier. Beneath the overhang of a leaning juniper she spotted a pile of shredded bark—perhaps a nest made by some kind of animal. In any case, the dry material would be the perfect fire starter.

She ducked under the branches and began to gather up the bark, folding up the hem of her shirt to form a carrying pouch. Nearby she could hear Mark walking around, getting the other fire materials ready. "I've found some great stuff here," she said. "We can get the fire going quick."

"There's not going to be any fire," said a deep voice behind her, and a beefy hand closed over her arm.

Chapter Eight

A woman's scream rose above the staccato report of gunfire, freezing Mark in his tracks. He dropped the armful of wood he had gathered and looked over his shoulder in the direction of the sound. Erin struggled with Cantrell beneath the branches of a leaning juniper, looking small and fragile in the big man's grasp. Mark turned to go to her, but bullets thudded into the trunk of a pine tree inches from his face, splinters and the sharp scent of pitch filling the air. He jolted forward, animal instinct driving him to flee as more gunfire erupted around him, so close he heard the whistle of bullets past his ears.

He ran until his lungs burned and pain stabbed his side. The gunfire had long since ceased, but he still imagined someone pursuing him. Ducking behind a many-branched juniper, he bent at the waist, hands on his knees, fighting for breath. His ragged breathing competed with the sigh of wind in the branches overhead as the only sounds in this part of the woods. If anyone still pursued him, they did so stealthily.

The memory of Erin struggling with Cantrell taunted him. Why hadn't he stayed and fought for her? He still had the rifle. If he had stopped and studied the situation more closely he might have found a way to help her, instead of fleeing like a coward.

Maybe a trained soldier wouldn't have run from someone firing at them, but he was only a scientist. The thought did nothing to assuage his guilt. Now that he was safe, he knew he had to go back. He wouldn't leave Erin alone to suffer whatever punishment those thugs dealt out.

Cantrell and the others wouldn't expect him to return. They thought of him as weak and passive. He had done exactly what they had expected of him: he had run away. They would believe themselves safe now, since he posed no threat.

He hefted the rifle and checked that there was a bullet in the chamber, ready to fire. He wished he had an extra magazine. The one he had was oversize, capable of holding thirty bullets, only two of which were missing. In a firefight he wouldn't last long, but if he had to fire off only a couple of rounds…

He didn't have to ask himself if he could kill another human being. To protect Erin, he would do what he had to. After all, Cantrell and the other guards wouldn't think twice about killing him. They had told him so many times.

He moved east, toward where he believed the road must be. After fifteen minutes of bushwhacking through thick undergrowth he reached the narrow track, where dirt and rocks showed through the snow. Then he headed back the way he had run. Cantrell and his companion must have parked on this road before pursuing Erin and Mark into the woods. They wouldn't expect him to be waiting for them when they returned to their vehicle.

He spotted the Hummer much sooner than he had expected, parked in the middle of the road like a hulking black beast. There was scarcely room on the cliff side to open the passenger door, while the driver had less than a foot of roadway to maneuver on before a steep drop-off. Mark paused fifty feet away, hiding in the underbrush along the side of the road, watching the Hummer, but in five minutes of waiting he saw no signs of life around it.

He approached cautiously, rifle at the ready. He tried the driver's door and found it unlocked, but the guards had taken the key with them and he saw nothing of interest on the seats or floorboards. He shut the door gently and turned his attention to the front left tire. Kneeling beside it, he fished the nail scissors from his pocket. They were old-fashioned and sturdy, the blades dull from use but coming together in a needle-sharp point. He grasped the handles and drove the point into the tire, using all his force and burying it all the way to the looped handles.

At first he feared the scissors weren't long enough to do any real damage, but then he heard the satisfying hiss of air escaping and the tire began to deflate.

He moved to the other front tire, intending to work his way around to all four tires, but a high-pitched keening stayed his hand. He jerked his head up in time to see movement in the undergrowth on the other side of the car. Scuttling like a crab, he retreated down the road and into the trees, positioning himself so that he was well concealed, but still had a clear view of the parked vehicle. Within seconds he caught a glint of auburn hair, and then Erin stumbled forward, Cantrell close behind her. The other guard—the young kid who had started packing the lab supplies at the cabin, flanked them on the left.

"Help! Someone help me!" Erin screamed.

Cantrell's slap snapped her head back and left a red imprint against her pale cheek. "Shut up!" he ordered. "Nobody can hear you out here anyway." He dragged her toward the car.

"What are you going to do with me?" she asked, her voice strained.

"Not what I'd like to do, that's for sure," Cantrell said.

The younger guard moved past them toward the vehicle. "We got a problem," he called back over his shoulder as he neared the Hummer.

"What is it?" Cantrell asked, still holding tight to Erin.

"Flat tire." The younger guard gestured toward the sagging front end. "We must have driven over a nail or something."

"Then get busy and change it."

The young man shrugged, then slung the rifle over one shoulder and walked around to the back of the vehicle and opened the hatch. While he retrieved the jack, lug wrench and spare tire, Cantrell pushed Erin down onto a log. "Sit," he ordered.

She sat, and glared up at him. Her face was deathly pale, except for the bright red imprint of Cantrell's hand. Mark studied the guard through the gun sight and wondered what his chances were of hitting the man from here. Then Cantrell moved to join his coworker at the rear of the Hummer. "We've got some rope back here somewhere," he said. "I'm going to tie her up before she can cause any more trouble." He glanced over at Erin again. "Don't even think about trying to run away. I won't hesitate to shoot you." He patted the stock of the rifle he held. "And I'm a really good shot."

The younger man carried the spare tire and other items to the front of the car and began to work on the flat while Cantrell continued to rummage in the rear of the vehicle. Now, while neither was close to Erin, would be Mark's best opportunity to surprise them without hurting her. With agonizing slowness, he crept closer, placing each foot with ultimate care in order to keep from making a sound.

He was less than ten yards from Cantrell when the guard straightened. "Found it," he said, holding up a coil of thin rope. "Now I'm going to deal with you."

He took a step toward Erin, but it was his last step. Mark fired and red bloomed in the man's chest. He stumbled backward, clutching at the wound, then dropped to his knees and pitched over in the snow. Mark swiveled toward the other guard, who gripped his weapon and looked around wide-eyed. Mark's shot caught him in the thigh, making him stagger. The young man dived off the road, into the ravine below.

Erin jumped up and looked around. "Over here!" Mark shouted, and motioned to her. She spotted him and started walking toward him, then running. He took her arm and urged her forward, adrenaline lending strength to his movements.

They ran wildly, not caring about the noise they made, crashing through the forest. They didn't stop until they reached a small clearing, where the bright sunlight streaming down seemed almost disconcerting after the darkness of the woodland. Mark stopped on the other side of the clearing and looked back. The woods were completely still, giving no indication of pursuit.

"Do you think they'll come after us?" she asked, sagging against a tree beside him, chest heaving as she gasped for breath.

"Not right away. I'm pretty sure the first guy I shot—Cantrell—is dead, and the other one is injured. The car is out of commission, at least until they change that tire. It will take a while for the young guy to regroup and get word to the others."

"They'll keep looking," she said.

"Yes." Mark turned to her. "Are you okay?"

"I don't know. I mean yes, I'm not hurt, and I'm still alive. That's something."

He touched the mark on her face, which was beginning to fade. "When he hit you, I wanted to make him pay. I never thought of myself as a killer, but…"

She grasped his wrist. "You're not a killer. You did what you had to do to save us. You know either one of them would have killed both of us without even blinking."

"You're right." But that didn't mean he wouldn't have nightmares about taking another life. "Come on." He straightened. "We have to keep moving. We still have a long way to go before we're safe."

"How far do you think?" she asked.

He didn't want to tell her they probably had many miles to go. She already looked to be on her last legs. "We'll probably be there by tomorrow," he said. "If we can keep parallel-ing the road."

"Tomorrow?" She seemed near tears.

"We'll find a safe place to spend the night," he said. Right now, even more than food, they needed rest and a break from the constant stress. Maybe they could find a cave, or an old mine shaft. Anything to get out of the wind and try to let their bodies recover a little.

ERIN TRUDGED ALONG behind Mark, all her efforts focused on putting one foot in front of the other. As they moved through the woods, they tried to keep the road in sight, since it was the only sure way down the mountain. Every few minutes a shudder ran through her and she looked back over her shoulder, expecting to see one of Duane's men coming after her.

Maybe Mark was right and she was suffering from a kind of PTSD. Maybe that even explained why her mother insisted on staying with Duane. Erin didn't see how anyone could love a man who was so intent on destroying others. But what did she know about love? She had never been married, or even had a serious lover.

"What first attracted you to your wife?" she asked Mark.

He glanced at her, his surprise at the question evident. "What do you mean?"

"What was it about her that made you want to be with her?" she asked. "Out of all the female students and women you worked with that you encountered every day, what made her the one you wanted for your wife?"

"She was beautiful, and very different from me. And she pursued me." He stepped over a fallen branch. "I never would have worked up the nerve to ask her out first."

"Was that important—that she be different from you?" Erin asked. "I always thought the things people had in common brought them together."

"I told you before—I'm not good at relationships. I'm too impatient with other people, too inward focused—selfish, really."

He hadn't been impatient with her. And he had risked his life to turn back and save her, not the act of a selfish man. "You're thoughtful and intelligent," she said. "You don't strike me as a man who acts rashly. That's not the same as being selfish."

"Christy wasn't like me. She was outgoing. Generous. She reveled in luxury. When we married she said my decorating style was 'dorm room aesthetic.' She turned our home into a warm retreat. I appreciated those things about her, even if I didn't always understand her."

Erin caught the wistful note in his voice. "I didn't mean to make you sad," she said. "I'm only trying to understand what brings a couple together. My mother always says she loves Duane, but I can't understand how that could be possible."

"People who knew me and my wife probably wondered what we were doing together," he said. "She could have had any man on campus that she wanted. For whatever reason, she chose me."

Maybe that was all love really was, Erin thought. Two people who needed each other. Mark had found a woman who overlooked his reticence and she had gained the home and security she craved. No wonder Erin had never had a serious relationship. She had spent most of her life learning to not need anyone.

"When we get out of here, I'm going to tell the police everything I know about Duane and his followers," she said. "Even if it means hurting my mother, I can't let him keep escalating his bizarre plans. Next time he might find a less ethical scientist to work for him."

"Yes. We have to make sure there's no next time."

"I won't let him capture me again, either," she said. "I couldn't bear it." The murderous look in the guard's eyes when he had slapped her would haunt her for a long time to come.

"We won't let him get to us again," Mark said. "I'll fight with everything I have to keep that from happening." He glanced at her. "But I really think the worst of our ordeal is over. We've got a big head start on the guards who were hunting us, and it's going to take them a while to regroup."

She wanted desperately to believe him, to believe they were almost safe again. She was about to say as much when something soft and wet hit her cheek. She wiped away the moisture. "I guess things can get worse after all," she said, then bit her bottom lip to keep from bursting into tears—or hysterical laughter.

"What are you talking about?" Mark asked.

"It's snowing." She looked up, and the swirl of white looked like a lace curtain settling over them. "We don't have to worry about Duane and his men finding us. We're going to freeze to death first."

Chapter Nine

The snow fell wet and heavy, melting on their clothes and bare skin. The clouds had foretold a storm all morning, but knowing it was coming hadn't really prepared them for the onslaught. Mark shoved his hands in the pockets of his jacket and hunched his shoulders against the icy wind and damp flakes. Erin huddled against him, her teeth chattering. "This snow just might save us," he said. "The guards will have a harder time following us, and it will cover our tracks."

"They might have a harder time following, but we're going to have a harder time moving, too." She tilted her head back to look up at the gray sky, snowflakes drifting down over her.

"Come on." He put a hand to her back. "We'd better get moving. That will warm us up, too."

Though already he could feel the damp chill settling in.

They kept to the edge of the road, pausing often to listen for the rumble of engines or nearby voices. But a deep, muffling silence had descended with the snow, which fell in a white curtain, already almost obscuring the road, and settling in clumps on the bushes and trees around them. "Do you remember how long you traveled on this road after you turned off the highway when they brought you here?" Mark asked.

"I think we were on a series of roads like this for a while," she said. "I remember a lot of bouncing around over rough ground and a lot of turns or curves. But I was blindfolded and disoriented, so I can't be sure. I thought they were taking me out in the wilderness to kill me, or to abandon me and leave me for dead."

The tremor in her voice made Mark tighten his hands into fists. If he did nothing else once he was free, he would see that Duane Braeswood paid for the suffering he had caused Erin and others like her.

"Did you ever hike in this area before?" she asked as they negotiated a narrow passage around a grouping of boulders.

"Nothing around here looks familiar," he

said. "I think we're farther south than I ever ventured. Old mining claims like the one we were on are all over the place in that part of the state. People use them as summer retreats, but the roads don't get much use in the winter."

"Too bad for us. If we could flag down a tourist, they would probably have a cell phone we could use."

"Phones might not work up here," he said. "I haven't seen any cell towers and companies don't have much incentive to build them in an area with so few people."

"Then I'd settle for a ride in some tourist's car to a town with working phones and police."

"I guess it doesn't hurt to dream," he said.

They fell silent again, only the sounds of their breathing or the occasional shifting rocks beneath their feet disturbing the winter stillness. Had the guards stopped their search, or moved to another area? Or were they even now scanning with infrared scopes, looking for the moving outlines of heat amid the cold that would give away their position?

"We're going to have to risk walking on the road for a while," he said when they came to a section with a wall of rock on one side and a drop-off on the other. "We'll duck back into the woods as soon as we can."

She said nothing, but followed as he dropped down onto the road, discernible only as a flat, white track alongside the cliff, the dirt surface completely obscured by an ever-deepening carpet of white. They rounded a curve and something darted from the rocks ahead. Erin's hand tightened on his arm, then she relaxed. "That rabbit scared me half to death," she said.

He looked down at the rifle, which he had instinctively brought into firing position. "No one could blame us for being jumpy," he said. He scanned the area, trying to make out anything unusual in the whiteness. They moved forward again, though he kept both hands on the rifle, ready to fight for his life and hers.

Behind him, Erin stumbled. "What the...?"

He turned. "Are you all right?"

"I'm fine." She held up a round, red reflector on the end of a three-foot long rod. "I tripped over this. Why do you think it's up here?"

"Maybe it's marking a culvert or some other hazard." He moved toward her, scanning the area.

"I've seen these at the ends of people's driveways." She started to toss the marker aside, but he took it from her, his heart thudding at her words.

"I think that's exactly why this is here,"

he said. "Marking a driveway leading to one of those mining claims I told you about." He scanned the roadside and spotted the opening in the trees. Only about eight feet across, the space was cleared of trees and brush and dipped down below the level of the road. "Come on." He took her arm and pulled her toward the drive.

She dug in and refused to move. "Where are we going?"

"If it is a claim, it might have a cabin," he said. "We need shelter to warm up, and they might have food, too."

"You just said the magic words. Let's go."

They stumbled down the steep, narrow track, snow falling hard enough now to obscure their vision and slow their progress. But at least the storm would cover their tracks. Mark had taken the reflector with him. If Duane's men didn't already know about this place, they weren't likely to find it now.

"I don't see any cabin," Erin said when they had traveled about a hundred yards. They were well below the level of the road now, out of sight of anyone passing by.

"This drive has to lead to something," he said. Maybe they would find only someone's campsite, or an old mine dump. But at this point, when he could no longer feel his fingers or feet, he would settle for any kind of temporary shelter. If they didn't get warm soon, they risked frostbite. And spending the night in this storm meant the real possibility of freezing to death.

They trudged on, the track gradually leveling out. Then he spotted the cabin ahead. Painted a dull green and almost obscured by trees as it was, he might have walked right past if he hadn't been so intent on searching for it. "Is that what I think it is?" Erin asked, stopping beside him.

"Let's go find out."

The cabin was even smaller than the one where he had been held prisoner, and looked much older, the paint dulled by weather and streaked with moss. Heavy wooden shutters covered the windows, and a stout padlock secured the door. They walked all around the building, but Mark couldn't see a way inside.

Erin hugged her arms across her chest and stamped her feet, visibly shivering. "Can we break in?" she asked.

"I could shoot off that lock, but the sound of gunfire carries a long way," he said. "It could lead Duane's men right to us."

"What about the windows?" She looked

around them. "There must be some way to pry off those shutters."

He spotted a shed a short distance away. It proved to be a combination outhouse and woodshed. Far in the back, he found an ax, the blade red with rust. Hefting it, he returned to the cabin. "Stand back," he said. "I'm going to try to wedge the blade under one of the shutters."

He moved to the back of the house, so the damage wouldn't be visible to anyone approaching down the drive. He found a gap at one corner of a wooden barrier, inserted the blade and put all his weight into pulling back on the ax. The wood gave way with a groan he hoped was muffled by the storm. Working the blade along the edge, he managed to pry away the entire shutter.

Erin tried to shove up the window sash, but it refused to budge. "It's stuck."

He peered over her shoulder. "I think it's nailed shut." He pointed to the heads of large nails visible on the inside sill.

She muttered a curse and pounded her fist against the window. "I don't want to steal anything, people," she said. "I just want to get warm."

Mark hefted the ax once more. "Stand back. I'm going to break the glass."

The pane shattered into dozens of shards that glittered on the snow before the fast-falling flakes obscured them. Mark wrapped his hand in his jacket and knocked out the remaining shards, then reached in and managed to grab hold of the nail head. He pulled and the nail slid out. Erin stared. "How did you do that?"

"It was probably designed to come out so whoever lived here could open the window for ventilation," he said. "Let me get the others." The remaining nails also slid out with little protest. Mark turned back to Erin. "Come on. I'll boost you inside, then I'll climb in after you."

THE CABIN SMELLED of dust and rodents. Erin tried not to think of all the mice—or worse—that might be living here as she moved away from the faint light streaming through the uncovered window, into the dark interior. She stumbled against something and felt along the back of a sofa, then turned to see Mark climb in after her. He was still carrying the ax, and leaned it against the wall beneath the window.

"We need to find a light," she said.

He lit a match, which illuminated grim surroundings—a sofa so faded the pattern of the upholstery was indiscernible, two wooden bunks along one side wall and a table and two chairs along the other wall. A two-burner camp stove and a metal bucket sat on the table and above that hung a wooden box with assorted canned goods, the labels worn and faded. Next to the canned goods sat a camping lantern. Mark crossed to this and lit it, the golden glow making Erin feel a little less desolate, if not any warmer.

A large, shallow box of sand occupied the middle of the room. Erin studied it. "Someone's idea of a cat box?" she asked.

"Probably for a woodstove." Mark pointed to a square of galvanized tin tacked to the ceiling. "That's probably covering where the stovepipe exited the room."

"Just our luck the stove is gone." She dragged one finger through the layer of dust on the table. "I don't think anyone has been here in a long time," she said.

"No. But that's something in our favor, I think." He slid the rifle from his shoulder and set it beside the ax beneath the window. "Let's find something to plug this broken pane."

She unearthed a towel from a box beside the bunks and he stuffed it in the broken window, blocking the draft, though the cabin remained cold. "I'm tempted to start chopping up chairs and build a fire anyway," she said.

He moved to the end of the bunks and pulled off a rolled-up sleeping bag. "Bundle up in this while I check out the canned goods," he said. "If there's propane for the camp stove, we can at least have something hot to eat."

She unzipped the sleeping bag and shook it out, grateful to see no signs of mice. Wrapping it around her, she settled on the sofa and watched as he sorted through the cans on the shelf above the table. "Beef stew, chili or chicken noodle soup?" he asked.

"Soup." She burrowed deeper into the sleeping bag, still shivering.

She closed her eyes, the sounds of him opening cans and shuffling pots lulling her not to sleep, but into a kind of frozen daze. The sleeping bag smelled of mildew and wood smoke, the scents transporting her to a long-ago camping trip with her mother and Duane. She had been fifteen, and had wanted to be anywhere but in the woods with a man she already despised. What her mother had promised would be a fun getaway turned out to be Duane's idea of survival training—sleeping on the ground in army surplus camping gear, cooking over a campfire and enduring daylong hikes that were more like forced marches.

When she had complained, he had threatened to leave her behind with only a compass and a sleeping bag to find her way home on her own. Her mother had watched, tight-lipped and wide-eyed, as Duane berated Erin, but the unexpected appearance of a trio of other hikers had prevented him from carrying out the threat, and Erin had reluctantly trailed after him all the way back to Duane's car.

"This should warm you up." Mark handed her a tray on which sat a bowl of fragrant soup and a steaming mug.

Erin balanced the tray on her lap and warmed her hands around the mug, inhaling deeply of the rich aroma of the contents. "Chocolate." She almost sang the word, and grinned at him.

He settled beside her and dug into his own bowl of soup. "There's enough food and bottled water here that we could hold out for several days if we have to," he said.

"We'll have to leave eventually." She touched the collar at her neck. "We can't linger too long." Duane had said the bomb would go off in a week, which left, what—five days? So little time.

"We'll leave as soon as we can," he said. "But not until the storm is over. For now, we've got a safe place to spend the night and regroup."

They ate in silence until their bowls and cups were empty. Erin set her dishes on the floor beside the sofa and burrowed deeper into the sleeping bag. "I feel so much better," she said. "I don't know how much longer I could have gone on out there."

"You and me both." He carried their dishes to the table, then retrieved the sleeping bag from the second bunk and settled in beside her with it wrapped around him. Though many layers of cloth separated them, the position felt somehow intimate.

"About what happened earlier," she said. "That kiss…" The memory of his lips on hers had haunted her all day and she had to clear the air.

"I'm not going to apologize for that," he said. "My timing may have been lousy, but I'm not sorry it happened."

"I don't expect you to apologize," she said. "And I'm not sorry it happened, either. I just wondered why you kissed me."

"Does a man need a reason to kiss a woman he's attracted to?"

She shifted, as if simply changing position could somehow make her comfortable with this awkward conversation. "I meant, why are you attracted to me? Is it just because you've been alone so long? Or do I remind you of your wife?" Erin bit her bottom lip, dreading the answer to her question, but needing to know.

"Maybe part of it is because I've been alone awhile, but I like to think I'm a little more evolved than that. I'm not attracted to you simply because you're a woman. As for my wife— no, you don't remind me of her." He sounded almost angry.

"I didn't mean to upset you," she said.

"I'm only upset that you seem to think so little of yourself. That I couldn't be attracted to you just because you're you. It's not only that you're beautiful, but you're strong. I was ready to give up on my life, and you showed me I still have so much to live for."

She looked away. She didn't feel strong most of the time. Yes, she had endured a lot, but she hadn't really had a choice. And as for her looks, they hadn't brought her anything but attention she had never wanted.

He leaned over her and gently took her chin in his hand and turned her head until she was looking into his eyes. "It's my turn to ask you why you kissed me back."

"Because you're the first man I've met in a long time who I felt I could trust." She said the words before she could stop them, and the truth of them shook her.

"You thought I was working for Duane," he said. "You came into that cabin already hating me."

"You convinced me I was wrong."

"How did I do that?"

He had let her glimpse his vulnerability before he showed her his strength. But she didn't know how to say that without embarrassing them both. "You didn't take advantage of me when you could have. You stood up to Duane's thugs. And I believed your story. I've spent a lot of years seeing through lies, and I believe you've been telling the truth."

"Then why don't you believe me when I say I'm interested in you because you're you? I feel a connection to you I haven't felt with anyone for a very long time."

"I was afraid to believe you because I wanted so badly for it to be true."

He caressed her cheek. "What about our bad timing? We're not in the best circumstances for romance."

"If everyone waited for everything to be perfect before they began a relationship, a lot more people would be alone." She didn't want to be alone anymore—not when she had no idea how much time they might have left. She grabbed the front of his jacket and pulled him to her, crushing her mouth to his. For once she allowed herself to be greedy, taking what she wanted.

His fervor matched hers, two hungry exiles suddenly presented with a feast. Tongues tangled, lips twined, hands explored. She dragged down the zipper of his jacket and slid her hands beneath his sweatshirt, over the firm plane of his abdomen and the hard muscles of his chest. She brushed fingertips through the dusting of hair on his chest, delighting in the beautiful maleness of him.

He helped her out of her coat, then coaxed off her sweater. His lips traced the curve of her breasts, his tongue sliding silkily down the valley between them. Then he peeled aside the lace of her bra and drew the hard bead of her nipple into his mouth.

She gasped and arched against him, the pull of his mouth reaching all the way to her sex. She twined her fingers in his hair, holding him to her, then dragged his head up to kiss him once more. With one hand, she groped behind her for the clasp of her bra and released it.

His eyes followed her movements as she sent the lacy garment sailing over the back of the sofa. "I've heard that cuddling naked in a sleeping bag is a good way to keep from freezing to death," she said.

"I've heard that, too. But I don't think we're in danger of freezing to death."

"I don't know about that. I'm pretty cold." She pressed her naked chest against his, reveling in the warmth and the delicious contrast of hard to soft, rough to smooth.

He caressed her arm and kissed the top of her shoulder. "I have a confession," he said.

"Oh?"

"I've wanted to be naked with you since the day the guards threw you into that cabin with me."

"Mmm." She traced her tongue along his collarbone. "I wanted that, too. Well, maybe not right away. It took me a few hours."

"Then we have a lot of time to make up for," he said.

"I like the way you think." She reached for the zipper of his pants, but he grabbed her wrist to stop her.

"I hate to be the one to point this out," he

said. "But there probably isn't a condom within miles of this place."

Knowing he had even thought of protection made her want him that much more. She racked her brain, rationalizing their situation. "We don't have to worry about disease," she said. "I'm healthy and I haven't been in a relationship for a couple of years."

He stroked her cheek. "Are the men where you live blind or crazy?"

She shook her head. "Neither. It was my choice." Though she had been physically intimate with a few men over the years, she had never allowed any of them to get emotionally close, and she had always ended relationships after a few weeks or months. Anything more was too dangerous. She had never felt as connected to a man—or as safe—as she did with Mark now.

"I haven't slept with a woman since my wife." He wrapped a strand of Erin's hair around his finger. "Are you on birth control?"

She pressed her forehead to his and sighed. "No such luck."

The dance of his fingertips up her spine sent a flutter through her. "There are a lot of things we can do short of actual intercourse." He cupped her breast and her breath quickened.

"I'm listening," she whispered.

He kissed the tender spot beneath her jaw. "I want to be intimate with you in whatever way we can."

She took hold of his zipper once more. "I want that, too."

A need to linger and savor replaced their earlier haste, as if they were both silently acknowledging that, no matter what the uncertain future brought, they would sear this interlude into their memories. They helped each other out of their clothes, then pressed their bodies together, naked beneath the sleeping bags.

"I'm warmer already," she said, and wrapped her legs around his hips, his erection nudging at her entrance, both teasing and thrilling her.

He trailed his hands down her back, then cupped her bottom, caressing, sending a shimmer of fresh arousal to her core. When he shifted his attention to the front of her thighs, she obliged by moving apart from him enough to allow his hands between them, his fingers tracing around her entrance, then delving in the folds above.

She arched into his palm as he slid one finger into her and began to stroke with his thumb, playing her like a skilled musician. When he lowered his mouth to her breast and began to suckle, she no longer felt tethered to the earth, instead soaring in a thrilling ride to unknown heights.

His hands and mouth coaxed sensations from her she had all but forgotten about—or never known. As she wrapped her arms around him, pulling him as close as possible, she battled the desire for this moment to never end, and her growing need for it to do so. When at last her climax crashed over her, his mouth claimed hers once more, muffling her cry of joy. She opened her eyes and met his gaze, the raw need reflected there sending a last shudder of completion through her. He withdrew his hand slowly and pressed a tender kiss to her temple.

"Your turn now," she said, and reached down between them to take him in her hand.

"You don't have to—" The sentence went unfinished as she slid down the length of his body and took him in her mouth.

He let out a low groan and caressed the back of her head as she teased him with her tongue and lips, delighting in her power to leave him speechless. She deepened the contact and felt him go inward, building toward his own release. A surge of fresh desire washed over her, a desire—no, a need—to give him this gift in such an intimate way. If being with him like this was so erotic and transforming, how incredible would actual intercourse be?

He gripped her shoulders and his body tensed. His climax shuddered through him, seeming to move through her body as well as his own. As soon as the last tremor left him he dragged her up beside him, cradling her head on his shoulder. Neither of them spoke for many minutes.

Eyes closed, sleep dragged at her, pulling her into welcome blankness. But before she succumbed, she wanted to say something, to let Mark know how much she cherished what they had shared together. She wouldn't be like a sappy teenager, declaring she was in love because she had had sex with a man. But being with him like this changed things, and she needed to acknowledge that. With sleep tugging at her, she fought to think clearly, to say something sincere but not too cloying.

What came out was less than articulate, more honest than she had wanted: "I never met a man who made me feel the things I feel with you," she said. "It scares me, but I don't want to run from that fear."

He caressed her back, stroking and massaging. "I've spent most of my life avoiding strong emotions," he said. "It was always easier to lose myself in facts and figures—things I could measure and control. I guess I was afraid, though I probably would have denied it if anyone had called me on it."

"Are you afraid with me?" Erin asked.

"No. With you it's as if I know there's nothing to be afraid of." His lips brushed her temple. "Try to get some rest. I think we're safe here."

Safe in his arms, she thought as she closed her eyes and settled more firmly against him. How ironic to find that kind of sanctuary now, when she had never faced greater danger.

MARK WOKE TO silvery moonlight streaming through the one uncovered window in the cabin, spilling across the sofa. The unfamiliar warmth and weight of Erin's body pressed against him made his throat tighten and his eyes sting. Days ago he had believed he had almost nothing left to live for. Now he had so much. He shifted so he could look at her, her face soft and somehow younger in her sleep, the worry lines that too often tightened her forehead banished for the moment.

His gaze shifted to the edge of the cruel collar that encircled her neck, and his jaw tightened. He would find a way to make Duane Braeswood pay for the suffering he had caused her. The collar was a particularly cruel torture, forcing her to live with the means of her own destruction.

Gently, hoping not to wake her, he lifted her chin to get a better look at the device. Maybe he could figure out how to undo that clasp, to free her of it. His hand stilled and ice water filled his veins as he stared at the band of metal, fully visible now. Where before the only item to draw the eye was the compact bomb affixed to the front, a new detail had emerged since they had fallen asleep. Now a digital readout glowed green in a black square next to the bomb. He watched as the numbers on the display changed, and he bit the side of his cheek to keep from shouting with rage.

"What's wrong? Why are you staring at me that way?"

Erin crossed her arms over her breasts and tried to pull away from him. He forced himself to assume a calmer expression. "It's okay," he said. "I didn't mean to scare you."

"What is it?" she asked again. "Something's wrong. I can see it on your face."

He gestured to her collar. "That…thing. The bomb. It has a timer."

"A timer?" She sat up straighter and put one hand to the metal.

He took the hand and cradled it in his own. "You can't feel it," he said. "It's a digital read-out. It wasn't there before. It was either programmed to show up now, or Duane set it off remotely."

"What's it doing? What does it say?" Erin pulled her hand from his and tugged at the metal band, as if she might tear it away from her neck.

He stared at the glowing green numbers that slowly ticked off the seconds. "It's counting down time. Maybe time until the bomb goes off."

She clutched at him. "How much time do I have?"

"We. I'm not going to leave you alone with this."

"How much time?"

"Twenty-three hours and thirty-nine minutes."

Chapter Ten

"That can't be right," Erin said, panic like a giant hand gripping her heart. "Duane said the bomb wouldn't go off for a week."

"Maybe he lied. Or he had the ability to reset the timer remotely."

She threw off the sleeping bag and reached for her clothing. "We have to leave now," she said.

"That's too dangerous," Mark said, but he began to pull on his own clothing. "It's pitch-dark out there and still snowing. If we try to leave now we'll get hopelessly lost and maybe freeze to death."

His words made sense, but this whole situation was beyond crazy. She couldn't respond to it logically. "We have to reach help before it's too late," she said.

He put a steadying hand on her shoulder.

When she raised her eyes to meet his she felt bathed in his calm determination. "We'll leave as soon as it's light enough to do so safely," he said. "Meanwhile, we can spend the time gathering supplies and getting ready."

"All right." She took a deep breath. Everything was far from all right, but maybe she could hold on if she pretended it was. "What do we need to do?"

"I'll start by fixing a hot meal."

"I couldn't eat."

"This isn't about appetite. It's about survival. You'll stay warmer and keep going longer if you get some calories in you."

While he heated canned chili, she rolled up the sleeping bags and the blankets from the bunks. When he summoned her to the table she forced herself to choke down the food, which might have been sawdust in hot water for all she could taste. As she ate, all her attention was fixed on the band around her throat and the digital display she couldn't see that was ticking down the minutes until her destruction.

Mark did his best to keep her distracted. While he rigged a makeshift knapsack out of an old hunting shirt he found hanging by the front door, he had her gather the rest of the canned food, a can opener and matches to go into it.

When the sun was far enough up in the sky for them to clearly see their way, they climbed out the back window of the cabin. "We're bound to intersect a main road within an hour or two," he said. "I don't think there's any place in the state where we would be farther from civilization than that."

"I hope your brother knows some fast—and close—bomb experts," she said.

"He's FBI. They have experts on everything."

"Great." She did her best to sound optimistic, but Mark must have seen through her bluff. He patted her back.

"We're going to get through this," he said. "Come on."

If she hadn't been so miserable over the bomb and their chances for escape, she might have enjoyed the hike through the snow-covered woods. Last night's storm had left the world draped in a white coverlet that sparkled in the early morning sunlight. But the same snow that made the world look soft and beautiful all but obscured the drive leading up to the road, and left them both wet to the knees from trudging through it. Worse, when Erin looked back over her shoulder, their tracks stood out clearly in the smooth white surface.

Mark joined her in staring at the signs of their passage. "There's nothing we can do about that," he said. "We just have to keep moving and stay ahead of them."

They set out again and were both soon breathing heavily as they made the steep ascent to the road. Mark climbed up first, then turned to pull her up alongside him. A new wave of dismay washed over her as she stared at the sight before them. Twin tire tracks cut through the thick drifts, compressing the snow and making it clear that at least one large, capable vehicle had passed this way recently. "They haven't given up searching for us," she said, if only to break the stillness that threatened to smother them.

"We knew they wouldn't."

Yes, she knew Duane's men wouldn't stop until they found her and Mark, but some small part of her—the part apparently given to fantasies—had hoped they would tire of the search, or give them up for dead. This proof of how close their pursuers were shook her badly.

"Come on." Mark adjusted the makeshift pack and set off along one of the tire tracks.

She hurried after him. "Why are you walking in the middle of the road?" she asked.

"We can move faster on the packed snow. They probably already know we're up here, so all we can do is hope to outrun them."

"Why do you think they know we're here? I mean, they know we're somewhere, but they can't be sure we're right here."

She couldn't help thinking a touch of pity lurked beneath the sympathy in his expression. "I'm beginning to think there's some kind of tracking device on that collar. Setting off that timer last night, when we were stopped and thought we were at least momentarily safe, seems like the kind of mind game Duane enjoys playing."

"So what is he going to do now? Let us stumble around in the snow for a while, then swoop down and capture us once more?"

"I don't know." His expression grim, Mark clutched the rifle. "But I'm not going back with them. And I'm not going to let them take you, either, not if I can help it." He gestured in the direction they were headed. "All I know is this road goes somewhere and if we can get there before they do, we can call for help."

She fell into step behind him. He was right—they could move faster on the packed snow, and the width of the road allowed them to walk side by side. The track led steadily downhill, and she began to feel more optimistic. After half an hour or so, they spotted a signpost ahead. "Windrow, four miles," Mark read.

"Have you ever heard of Windrow?" she asked.

"No, but if it's big enough to warrant a road sign, they probably have a phone. We can be there in an hour."

The thought of being only an hour away from rescue—even knowing it would probably be several hours after their phone call before help actually arrived—was enough to add wings to her feet. They hurried along and within another half hour reached a paved road and a second sign pointing the way to Windrow.

"I can't believe we're almost there." She squeezed Mark's arm and they grinned at each other. She forgot all about her wet, cold feet and frozen cheeks, anticipating hot coffee and a safe place to rest and share their story. This whole crazy ordeal would soon be over.

Mark opened his mouth to reply, then froze, the smile melting from his face. "Do you hear that?" he whispered.

Her stomach twisted as the distinct roar of an engine moving down the grade behind them grew louder.

MARK GRABBED ERIN'S arm and pulled her toward woods alongside the road as bullets ripped into the snow at their feet. The explosion of gunfire echoing off the surrounding rocks drowned out her screams as he pushed her behind him and slid the rifle off his shoulder.

The Hummer slid to a stop at the end of the road, the long barrels of assault rifles protruding from the front window and over the top of the vehicle, pointing toward where the two fugitives hid in the underbrush. Mark crouched in front of Erin, sighting along the barrel of his rifle. The moment he fired, the men in the vehicle would know exactly where they were hiding—but they might know that already. If he could kill one of them before they killed him, he might give Erin a chance to get away.

The world erupted with the sound of gunfire as a barrage of bullets strafed the roadside, ending only inches from their hiding place. Erin pressed her face against Mark's back. He could feel her trembling, but she remained silent. His own heart pounded so hard he thought it might burst. Tightening his hold on the rifle, he forced himself to inhale deeply and exhale slowly. The next barrage of gunfire would probably find them. He couldn't wait any longer.

He sighted in on the driver, the man's head clearly visible in the open window of the Hummer. Mark took another deep breath, held it, then depressed the trigger.

He had heard men say that in moments like this everything happened in slow motion, but for Mark, time seemed to speed up. The driver's body jolted from the impact of the shot, while the man on the other side of the car swung the barrel of his rifle in their direction. The man managed to get off one shot before Mark fired on him, too. Splinters of rock flew up, momentarily blinding him, but when his vision cleared, the man on the other side of the car was no longer visible and the vehicle was still.

"You've been hit!" Erin spoke softly, but her words conveyed her horror.

She reached for him, but he shrugged her off. "Don't move," he ordered. "There might be a third man in the car." The motion sent pain shooting down his arm, and he felt the hot stickiness of blood trickling from his shoulder.

But he blocked out the pain, focused on the Hummer. Nothing moved, though the rough grumbling of the idling engine drowned out any sounds that might have come from inside the vehicle.

"Are they dead?" Erin asked.

"I don't know."

"How are we going to find out?"

He didn't know that, either. Now that the first rush of adrenaline was fading, his arm throbbed and he was having trouble thinking clearly. "One of us will have to go out there, I guess."

"I'm not letting you go." Before he could stop her, she inched forward, but she didn't, as he had feared, move toward the vehicle. Instead, she took the rifle from him and fired on the Hummer. The shots were wild, pinging into the back fenders and flattening one of the tires.

Mark's ears still rang from the blasts as he let out his breath in a rush. Nothing moved in or around the vehicle. He shoved to his feet, swaying a little as he did so. Erin moved beside him, supporting him. "You need to see to that wound," she said.

"When we're safe." He took a step forward, jaw clenched, determined not to falter or pass out. "We have to get out of here."

"How?" She looked toward the still-idling Hummer, which listed to one side on the flat tire.

"We'll have to walk."

When Mark stepped out onto the road, he braced himself for the onslaught of bullets. When no shots were fired, the second step was easier. "Wait here while I check the car," he said.

She opened her mouth to argue, but he cut her off. "Do you really want to see what's inside there?"

She pressed her lips together and shook her head. He took the rifle back from her and approached the car obliquely, gaze riveted to the interior, alert for any sign of movement. He saw the man outside the car first, and recognized the one Tank had addressed as Trey, sprawled in the road beside it, eyes staring vacantly at the sky.

The driver, another familiar face Mark hadn't bothered to name, slumped inside the car, his blood-streaked face resting on the seat, the gun lying across his chest. Mark reached inside the vehicle and switched off the ignition. In the silence that followed, he was aware of his own jagged breathing.

He moved away from the vehicle and signaled for Erin to join him. "They're dead," he said. "But we need to get out of here. There are at least three guards left who are probably still looking for us." And Duane had many more men at his disposal—foot soldiers he could send into the fray until Mark and Erin were either captured or destroyed.

"Let me take care of your wound or we won't get very far," she said.

He glanced down at his throbbing left arm, where a dark stain marked the sleeve. A wave of dizziness washed over him and he swayed.

Erin helped him to a rock beside the road, where he sat while she helped him out of his coat, then tore off the sleeve of his shirt. The wound was a perfectly round hole in his upper arm, the edges swollen and dark blood welling. Erin winced, but said nothing as she walked around to his other side and began pulling at his unbloodied shirtsleeve.

"What are you doing?" he asked.

"I need something to make a bandage to help slow the bleeding," she said. "That's all we can do until you see a doctor."

She managed to rip off the sleeve, then tore it into strips. She made a pad from some of the strips and wound another around the pad to hold it in place. With the final two strips she fashioned a makeshift sling, then helped him back into the coat, draping the left side over his shoulder. "How does that feel?" she asked.

"Better," he lied, and stood, fighting a wave of dizziness and nausea. "Let's get out of here."

ERIN RESISTED THE urge to reach out to support Mark, sensing he would push her away. He was in full-on tough guy mode right now, and maybe that was what was keeping him going. She tried to focus on safety ahead. Later, when she had put some distance between the events of the afternoon, she might be willing to contemplate how close they had come to death.

A green highway sign announced they had reached the Windrow town limits, but all Erin could see was more rock and trees—not the bustling community she had hoped for. "Do you think it's a ghost town or something?" she asked.

"I see a building up ahead." Mark put a hand to his eyes and squinted. "It looks like some kind of store." He started walking again. "They ought to at least have a phone, and right now, that's all I care about."

The store in question had a faded sign that read McCarty's over the green wooden door. The rest of the building hadn't seen a coat of paint in this century. A rusting newspaper box and a soft drink machine with "Out of Order" scrawled across the front with black marker took up most of the small front porch. The only attempt to spruce the place up was a dented milk can by the door into which someone had stuck a trio of fake sunflowers. The flowers drooped with a dusting of snow.

Mark paused in front of the door. "Just a minute," he said. He ducked around the side of the building. When he reappeared seconds later, he no longer had the rifle.

"What did you do with the gun?" she asked.

"I hid it in the bushes. I didn't want the store clerk to think we were robbers."

"Good idea."

He started for the door again, then froze, reaching for the doorknob.

"What's wrong?" Erin asked.

He nodded toward the newspaper box. "What's the date on that paper?"

She stared at it, the headline visible through the mesh door momentarily stopping her breath: Domestic Terrorist Group Claims Nuclear Bomb.

Mark bent to study the paper more closely. "It's today's date."

Erin crouched beside him and read aloud

the story beneath the bold headline: "'A group calling themselves the Patriots, believed to be based in the US, has threatened to detonate a nuclear bomb within twenty-four hours if their demands are not met.'" She looked up at Mark. "I can't read any more."

Mark jerked the handle of the machine, but it refused to budge. "Maybe we can find out more inside."

Erin stood, nausea rising in her throat. "You told me the bomb wasn't real," she said.

"It's not." His face was pale, but his eyes blazed. "There's no way he could have armed what I gave him. Not this soon." He took her elbow. "Come on. We've got to call my brother and find out what's going on."

The interior of the store smelled of pipe tobacco and old dust, but the heat blasting from a wall furnace made Erin feel better as soon as she stepped inside. A man with a frizz of iron gray curls and a bushy mustache looked up from behind the front counter as Mark closed the door behind them. "I didn't hear a car pull up," the clerk said.

"It's down the road a ways," Mark said. "We had a little trouble and we need to use your phone."

Erin had thought they would tell whoever

they encountered the truth—that they had been kidnapped by a madman, held prisoner in a remote cabin and escaped, after enduring a shootout with armed thugs. But she could see how deranged that might sound to a stranger, so she followed Mark's lead. "We just need to call my friend's brother to come pick us up," she said.

The old man stared at Mark's bandaged arm beneath the coat. "You in some kind of accident?"

"Yes, and I need to call for help."

The old man's expression didn't soften. "I haven't seen you two around before. Where are you from?"

"We're visiting the area," Mark said.

"Don't you have cell phones you can use?"

Erin bit back a groan of frustration. Why was this guy being such a pain about a simple request to use the phone? "We lost our cell phones," she said.

"What did you say your names were?"

"We didn't." Mark's expression was tight. Erin couldn't tell if he was in pain or merely annoyed.

"Please." She leaned across the counter toward the old man and gave him her most pleading look. "My friend is hurt and we really need help. We just need to use your phone for a few minutes."

He studied them a long moment, his expression unsympathetic. "All right," he finally said. "Come with me."

He led the way to a back room that was evidently used for storage. "The phone's back there," he said, pointing into the shadows.

"Back where?" Erin leaned forward, trying to see.

"It's on the rear wall."

Mark started into the room and Erin followed.

The door slammed, plunging them into darkness. "Hey!" she yelped.

Mark pounded on the door. "What do you think you're doing?" he shouted. "Let us out of here."

"Do you really think I'm that dumb?" Was the old man really *chuckling*? "A couple of guys stopped by this morning, said they were with the FBI and they were looking for a pair of fugitives. You two fit the description they gave me to a T. They said there was a big reward for your capture. So no, I'm not going to let you go."

Chapter Eleven

Mark squeezed Erin's arm, as much to reassure himself as to comfort her. Of all the places they might have ended up needing help, they had to wind up with a crazy man. "What did the two men you spoke with look like?" he called through the door. "Did they show you credentials?"

"They didn't need credentials. Who would make up a story like that? They were dressed in black and had big guns. They said you two were dangerous subversives who were part of this group that wants to blow up the country."

"We're not!" Erin protested. "They were lying."

"A guilty person would say that, wouldn't they?" The clerk's voice rose with indignation. "I'd rather take the word of the law than you.

They left their card. It says Federal Bureau of Investigation, right there in black-and-white."

"They weren't real agents if they didn't show you their badges and identification," Mark said. "I know because my brother is with the FBI."

"Sure he is. And I'm a monkey's uncle. I'm not as dumb as I look, mister. They said there's a big reward for the person who turns you in. I'm going to call them right now, and then I'm going to start planning my vacation." His footsteps retreated.

Mark pounded a fist against the door in frustration, but all this did was send a shock wave of pain through him. "You're making a mistake!" he shouted. "Let us out!"

"We're the good guys!" Erin said. "Please, let us out!"

In answer, rock music blared, the pounding of drums and screech of guitars drowning out their calls for help.

Light suddenly flooded the space. Surprised, Mark turned to Erin.

"There's a switch here by the door." She raised her voice to be heard over the blare of music and gestured to the light switch. "No reason we have to fumble around in the dark." She leaned toward him, frowning. "You're white as a sheet. Please sit down before you fall down." She took his good arm and led him to a stack of cases of soft drinks and pushed him down. She settled beside him. "How are you feeling?"

He felt like leftovers that had sat in the sun for too long, but saying so would only worry her. He gestured for her to lean close enough that he didn't have to shout over the blare of AC/DC. "The phony agents the old man talked to must have been Duane's men," he said. "He probably sent them to talk to everyone around here as soon as he learned we had escaped."

"Why is he trying to pass that bomb off as real if it isn't?" she asked. "And why now?"

"I don't know," Mark said. "Unless he feels like federal agents are getting too close to discovering him and this is a last mad dash for power."

"What are we going to do?" Erin asked. "If Duane's men show up here there's no telling what they'll do to us."

Mark had a good idea what Duane would do to them, and it wasn't pretty. By now the leader of the Patriots had to have figured out the bomb Mark had made was a dud, even if he was trying to persuade others that it was real. He would want revenge on Mark for trying to trick him, and Mark knew he wasn't a good enough actor to convince Duane that he was still on his side, so the madman would eliminate him. And the fact that Erin was his stepdaughter apparently meant nothing, so Duane would likely kill her, too.

"We have to get out of here before Duane's men show up," he said.

"How do we do that?"

He stood and began walking around the room. Cartons of toilet paper and cases of soda sat side by side with an old tobacco display, a kid's toboggan, a broken barbecue grill and even a set of balding tires. The room was windowless, though two of the walls were fashioned of painted cinder block, which indicated to Mark that they were probably outside walls. He looked up at the ceiling and his heart jumped as he recognized the outline of what might be a hatch leading to the attic. "Help me drag these tires over here," he said, tugging at the stack.

Erin rushed to help him. She followed his gaze to the ceiling hatch. "Do you think that leads outside?" she asked.

"It probably leads to the attic," he said. "But from there we might be able to access the roof, or another part of the store. It's the only exit besides the door, so it's worth a try." He scrambled onto the stack of tires, which put him within arm's reach of the hatch. But lifting both arms over his head was impossible. His shoulder muscles cramped in agony when he tried to raise his injured limb. He settled for shoving at the hatch with one hand. At least he didn't have to worry about anyone hearing them, with that music turned up to full volume. The hatch moved easily, and he shoved it aside far enough to allow a person to climb up into the space.

But that person wouldn't be him. With only one good arm, he wasn't going to be able to lift himself up there. He looked down at Erin, her anxious face upturned to him. "You'll have to climb up there and go for help," he said.

"I can't leave you!"

"You have to!" He squatted and took her arm. "And you need to move fast, before Duane's men get here."

"Where am I supposed to go?" she asked.

"Follow the road to the next town. There's bound to be one. Stay out of sight of traffic. You don't want to run into Duane's men headed here. Find a police station or a fire station or somewhere official, and call the number I'm going to give you." He glanced around them. "Find something to write with and I'll give you my brother's number. Once you tell him what's going on, he'll take over and send help for me."

"What if Duane gets to you before I can reach your brother?" she asked.

"I'll fight him. I'm not going to give up after coming this far. Now hurry."

She found a Sharpie and tore a piece of cardboard from one of the cartons. Mark wrote "Luke Renfro" and Luke's private number on the cardboard and handed it back to her. "Put that somewhere safe and climb up here. I'll boost you into the attic. Take whatever exit you can find, and once you get outside, start moving away from here as fast as you can. When Duane's men arrive, I'll stall them as long as I can."

She climbed onto the tires with him, the uneven platform forcing her to stand with her body pressed to his. "I don't want to leave you," she said, her hands braced against his chest.

"Right now, you're the only one who can save us." He clasped her close and kissed her, a fierce embrace that he hoped told her all he didn't have words to explain—how much she had come to mean to him in their short time together and how much he hated for them to part. He had his doubts about her being able to summon help before Duane did away with him, but at least Mark would die knowing she was safe.

He tasted the salt of her tears and broke the kiss. "Don't cry," he whispered, and wiped her cheek with his thumb.

She ducked her head. "I'd better go. Give me a boost."

Awkwardly, relying on his good arm, he helped her scramble onto his back and from there into the attic. Once she was safely away, he slid the hatch back in place, then shoved the tires into the corner. When the clerk and Duane's men did arrive, Mark wanted to give Erin as much time as possible before their pursuers figured out she had escaped.

With a groan, he sank to the floor, legs stretched out in front of him and back against a stack of boxes. All he could do now was wait, and pray that Erin, at least, reached safety.

ERIN CROUCHED IN the dark attic, the loud rock music from the front of the store vibrating the floorboards beneath her. The attic smelled of dust and mice. She suppressed a shudder, hoping no rodents were in residence at the moment. As her eyes adjusted to the dimness she could make out cardboard boxes shoved against the wall and a stack of old suitcases next to a metal floor lamp. The light seemed brighter to her right, so she moved in that direction, crouched over to keep from hitting her head on the rafters, and stepped carefully on the joists. The last thing she wanted was to crash through the ceiling onto the clerk's head.

She rounded a stack of boxes and a cry of relief escaped her as she recognized the dusty outline of a window. Hurrying to it, she wiped at the grimy glass with the sleeve of her jacket and looked down into the store's backyard. A sagging chain-link fence ran along the back and a rusted barbecue smoker sat in the shade of a barren tree. She stood on tiptoe and tried to see the ground and gulped. She guessed the drop was at least ten feet, maybe more, and though several inches of snow coated the ground, that wasn't enough to provide much of a cushion for her fall. If she was lucky, she'd escape with only a sprained ankle or a broken arm, but she didn't like the thought of risking that. Heart sinking, she turned away from the window to explore the rest of the attic.

The other end held no window, only a rusting metal vent that didn't yield when she pushed against it. The only other exit was the hatch over the storeroom, where Mark waited. The thought of him wounded and trapped spurred her on. She'd have to risk jumping out the window, but first she had to raise the sash or break the pane. She needed something to protect her from the broken glass. Maybe some old clothing or rags. She tugged at the lid of the nearest trunk and wrenched it open, coughing at the cloud of dust that rose. Trying not to think about mice, she tugged at what looked like cloth shoved inside the trunk, and yanked out a moth-eaten chenille bedspread that might have once been a bright blue, but looked like a stained gray in the dim light. The coverlet was easily large enough for a king-size bed, and its expanse gave her an idea.

She returned to the window, dragging the bedspread with her. While the music continued to shake the rafters, she hefted the metal floor lamp. Shielding her face with the cloth, she drove the lamp into the window like a spear, shattering the glass. Before she could lose her nerve, she tied one end of the bedspread to the rafter over the window and tested the knot with her weight. It held, so she cleared away as much of the loose glass as possible, and stuffed the rest of the anchored coverlet out the window, so that it trailed down the side of the house. Then she knelt on the sash, facing inward, took hold of the bedspread and began to climb down, bracing her feet against the weathered siding of the building and holding tightly to her makeshift rope.

The bedspread ended five feet from the ground, but that was close enough for her to feel comfortable jumping. She tried to yank the bedspread after her, but it held fast, so she was forced to leave it hanging from the open window. With luck, the clerk wouldn't decide to take a smoke break in the backyard and see it flapping in the breeze, giving her away.

After making sure the coast was clear, she climbed the fence, then hurried to the side of the house and retrieved the rifle from its hiding place in the bushes. She shouldered it, then crossed in back of a few buildings that appeared to be vacant. When she was sure she was out of sight of the store, she turned up toward the road. The wind had picked up, the icy breeze sending a chill through her, but the scent of snow and cedar invigorated her, and the need to reach help for Mark made her walk faster, which helped to warm her.

She had gone only a few yards when the whine of an approaching vehicle sent her scurrying for cover in the trees. Crouched low behind snowy branches, she studied the black Humvee headed into town. It wasn't the same car Mark had fired upon earlier, but it was very like it. And the wide shoulders and grim faces of the two men in the front seat of the vehicle sent fear shuddering through her. Those were two of Duane's men, she was certain. And in only a few minutes they would burst into that storeroom to take Mark away.

As soon as the vehicle passed, she began retracing her steps to the store. She didn't have time to get help from someone else. She would have to save Mark herself. She had the rifle, though she wasn't sure how much ammunition was left in the single clip, or how much good the gun would do her against both Duane's men and the store clerk, who might be armed, as well. She'd have to find another weapon, or get to Mark in the storeroom before the other three did.

Duane's two henchmen were just getting out of the Hummer when Erin looked around the side of the building toward them. Dressed in dark suits and sunglasses, they fit the television portrayal of federal agents, though they were considerably beefier than any of the supposed Feds she remembered. One reached in-

side his black overcoat and she caught the glint
of a handgun tucked under his arm. He looked
toward his cohort and nodded, and they strode
across the gravel lot and through the front door
of the store.

As soon as they were inside, Erin, crouching low, scooted across the yard to the vehicle. She peered in the passenger-side window,
hoping to spot another weapon or two. Duane's
goons almost always carried semiautomatic
weapons, and since the two phony FBI agents
hadn't been carrying any long guns, she hoped
to find them in the Hummer.

She spotted one rifle on the passenger floorboard in the back, but what met her gaze on the
driver's side front set her heart pounding not
with fear, but elation. The keys to the Hummer dangled from the steering column. The
massive vehicle, with its reinforced grill, four-
wheel drive and powerful engine, just might
be the best weapon at her disposal.

As the blaring music inside the store
abruptly died, Erin opened the passenger door
of the Hummer and slid inside, climbing over
the center console and sliding into the driver's
seat. Holding her breath, she twisted the key
and the engine turned over. Not hesitating, she
shifted into Reverse, backed up, then drove

around the side of the building. She floored the gas pedal as she sped toward the sagging chain-link fence. The jolt of impact with the fence thrust her back against the seat, but the Hummer rolled over the chain-link panel as if it was made of tinfoil. She kept right on driving, up to the corner of the building where the storeroom was situated. She backed up a foot or so, then stomped on the gas pedal, sending the Hummer crashing into the side of the store.

The cinder blocks and old plaster splintered against the vehicle's grille. She barely heard the shouts of the men as she drove into the building, where one of Duane's men had hold of Mark's arm. The image of the four men frozen with shock and gaping at her would remain burned into her memory forever. She aimed the Hummer toward Mark's captor and the man released him and dived out of the way, while Mark headed in the opposite direction.

Erin lowered the driver's side window. "Get in!" she shouted to Mark, then ducked beneath the dash as a bullet shattered the windshield.

Mark wrenched open the back door and dived inside. Staying low, Erin shoved the shifter into Reverse and screeched backward through the debris. By the time she reached the backyard, Mark was leaning over the backseat beside her, firing out the shattered front window toward their pursuers. The clerk and Duane's two men had staggered out of the shattered building like ants from a ruined hill, one of the thugs cradling his arm, the other firing his handgun toward the fast-retreating Hummer.

Erin made a sharp turn and the vehicle jounced over the rough ground to the road. The tires squealed as she wrenched them onto the pavement and barreled away from the store. She reached back and pulled her seat belt across her body as Mark struggled into the front passenger seat. "Are you okay?" she asked.

"My life may have flashed before my eyes when you came barreling toward me with this thing," he said, buckling his own seat belt. "I thought you were trying to run me down."

"I was trying to run over the goon who had hold of you," she said. "I trusted you to have enough sense to get out of the way."

"I don't think sense was on my side as much as good reflexes." He reached into the backseat and retrieved the rifle she had spotted earlier on the floorboard. He glanced over his shoulder in the direction they had come.

"Anyone back there?" she asked, though

a check of the rearview mirror showed only empty road behind her. She had a clearer view back there than she did through the spider-webbed glass, but she wasn't going to complain. Every mile that unrolled beneath her tires was a mile farther from the most immediate danger.

"Not yet, but that store clerk is bound to have some kind of vehicle, so they'll be after us soon."

"We'll still have a head start. All we have to do is get to some place large enough that Duane won't have influenced everyone. Then we can call your brother."

Mark shifted to face her. "How did you get hold of this Hummer? You were supposed to climb out of that attic and go for help."

"I didn't get very far down the road before I saw those two headed back for you. Even if I could have run all the way to the next town, I wouldn't have found help in time to save you."

"You could have gotten away," he said. "You didn't have to come back and save me."

"Yes, I did." She glared at him. "And I'm pretty insulted that you think I would do otherwise."

He shrugged. "No one would blame you."

"You would have come back for me," she

said. "In fact you already did that—when Duane's men recaptured me in the woods."

"This isn't about keeping score," he said.

"No, this is about working together to keep each other safe. We're stronger together than either of us is on our own."

He didn't deny it and she knew she was right. Now that the worst of the danger was past, a thrill ran through her at the idea that she had saved him. She had fought past almost-paralyzing fear to do something bold and daring, and they had come out on the other side all right. They really did make an incredible team.

"You still haven't told me how you ended up with this car," he said.

"Duane's goons left the keys in it when they parked in front of the store. I guess they didn't think there was anyone around to bother it. Maybe they wanted to be sure they could make a quick getaway. I was looking for a way to get you out of the storeroom before they got to you, and decided this was it."

"Good thing they were driving a Hummer and not a sedan." He leaned over and touched the side of her face. "You're bleeding. Some of the glass from the window, I think."

Before she could protest, he pulled a handkerchief from his pocket and dabbed at the warm wetness that trickled down the side of her face. The tender gesture sent a tremor through her and broke whatever toughness spell circumstance had cast over her. She gripped the steering wheel more tightly to control her shaking, and fought the nausea that welled in her throat. "I think it's just hitting me how close we came to dying back there," she said.

He squeezed her shoulder. "But we didn't die. We're going to be okay."

"Not if we don't get to your brother—and some explosives experts—soon." She touched the collar at her throat. "How much time do we have left?"

He glanced at her throat, and the display she couldn't see but knew was there. "We've got plenty of time," he said, but the concern in his eyes told a different story.

"How much time?" She lifted off the seat, trying to see her throat in the rearview mirror.

"Fifteen hours and nineteen minutes."

Fifteen hours. The words echoed in her head. She clung to the steering wheel, fighting a wave of dizziness.

"We're going to get help," Mark said. "We still have plenty of time."

"We don't know how much time we have before Duane sets off his bomb," she said. "Or whatever it is he's threatening everyone with."

Mark punched the radio button. "I'm going to see if I can learn anything more about that."

Bursts of static interspersed with crackling strains of music blared from the speakers as he spun the dial. Then a woman's solemn voice said, "…material recovered previously from the home where the Patriots' leader, billionaire Duane Braeswood, was believed to be living leads authorities to believe these threats are serious. Authorities are still searching for Braeswood and other people associated with his organization. Braeswood is described as a fifty-five-year-old white male, six feet tall, approximately one hundred and sixty-five pounds, with graying blond hair and blue eyes. Anyone with information as to his whereabouts and activities should contact the FBI."

The newscast shifted to a story about a professional athlete who had been arrested for assault. Mark switched off the station and sat back. "He's got to be bluffing," he said. "There's no way he armed that bomb."

"If people believe it's real, it doesn't matter." Erin tightened her grip on the steering wheel.

"He's making everyone afraid and they're all listening to him. He must be in heaven."

"The description they gave is what he used to look like," Mark said. "No one will recognize him from that. Someone who didn't know would see him now and think he's a harmless old man."

"We can tell the FBI what he really looks like, and that the bomb probably isn't real," she said. She would feel a lot better if she knew how far they were from help. "Look in the glove box and see if you can find a map," she said. "Maybe we can figure out where we are and where we should go."

"Better yet, this thing probably has GPS," Mark said. "That can help us find the closest police station."

She surveyed the dash. The array of dials and digital readouts resembled an airplane's cockpit. She didn't even recognize what half of the gauges were for. But there was one display that was familiar to her. Staring at it, she swallowed hard. "We have something else to worry about," she said.

"What is it?" Mark leaned over to get a better look at the dash. "Are we overheating? Do you think a bullet hit one of the tires?"

She shook her head and pointed to the gas gauge. "If we don't find a town soon, we're going to run out of gas and end up stranded."

Chapter Twelve

As if to confirm Erin's pronouncement, a chime sounded and an orange light on the dash flashed Low Fuel. Mark unbuckled his seat belt and leaned into the backseat.

"What are you doing?" Erin asked.

"I'm hoping Duane's men thought to carry an extra gas can, but I don't see anything back here. Do you remember seeing one strapped to the bumper or anything?"

"No. They probably planned to buy gas at the store before they left," she said.

"Which kind of defeats the purpose of a quick getaway." He settled into his seat once more. "Is Duane slipping on training his henchmen, or is good help hard to find for bad guys, too?"

"I think it's a sign he's getting too cocky," she said. "He's so sure he's going to win in the end that he thinks he can take shortcuts. Maybe that's all this threat with the bomb was—a shortcut to carrying out his 'vision.'"

"We need to find a shortcut," Mark said. He leaned toward the dash. "Let me see if I can find the GPS."

Much button pushing and second-guessing later, he figured out how to operate the GPS, which informed him they were eighteen miles from the nearest settlement, a mountain town large enough to boast a pizza place, three churches, a gas station, a medical clinic and a liquor store, but no police.

"At least we can get gas there," Erin said. "And maybe use the phone."

"How are we going to pay for the gas?" he asked.

She set her jaw. "We can start out begging, but if that doesn't work, we could assume the roles of modern day Bonnie and Clyde and hold up the place at gunpoint. That might be the quickest way for us to get to the police, and you can use your one phone call to get in touch with your brother."

"That's fine as long as we don't run into some trigger-happy local," he said. "Let's hope begging works."

The dashboard chimed again and she glanced

down. Mark followed her gaze to the warning light, which now glowed red. "We may not get a chance to beg or steal," she said, even as the engine coughed, sputtered, then died.

Erin steered the vehicle to the side of the road and rested her forehead on the steering wheel, eyes closed. "Now what?" she asked.

"We're back to walking."

"How long do you think it will take us to walk eighteen miles?" She sounded exhausted, as weary as he felt.

"It's more like fourteen or fifteen miles now," he said. "We can do it in five or six hours." Provided they didn't collapse before then. Or end up back in the clutches of Duane's men.

She lifted her head and her eyes met his. "Everything about this ordeal has felt impossible," she said. "Yet I keep on pushing forward. Maybe I'm just too exhausted to be afraid anymore."

"Or maybe you're a lot braver than you think." He leaned across the center console, ignoring the pain in his shoulder, to kiss her. Her warm sweetness revived him, the grip of her hand on his arm reminding him of all the reasons he had to keep fighting. "I'll never forget the sight of you behind the wheel of this

Hummer, barreling to my rescue," he said. "If you're strong enough to do that, you're strong enough to do anything."

"I don't know how much strength I have left," she said. "But I'm stubborn enough that I won't let Duane win. There's too much at stake to give up now." She opened the driver's side door. "Come on. We might as well start walking. I'd like to get to the next town before dark."

"Take one of the guns with you." He pressed one of the two semiautomatic rifles that had been stashed in the Hummer's backseat into her hands, along with an extra clip of ammunition, and collected the other rifle and ammo magazine for himself. "We'll have to leave the one we took from the cabin behind, since it doesn't have an extra ammo clip."

"What else do they have that we can use?" She opened the door to the backseat and he moved to the rear hatch. A quick scan of the vehicle's contents revealed a gallon jug of water, two blankets, a toolbox filled with miscellaneous hand tools and a first aid kit. The glove box yielded two protein bars.

"These look like they've been in here awhile," Mark said, handing her one of the bars.

"I'm so hungry I would eat a picture of food," she said, ripping the wrapper off the bar.

He bit into his bar and chewed. It was the consistency of jerky and tasted like sawdust, but it might be enough to keep them going a few miles farther. Once they were safe again, he planned to order the biggest steak dinner he could find. And pie. Peach pie. With ice cream. He shook his head, banishing the distracting fantasy.

He opened the first aid kit and found a packet of pain relievers and swallowed them down with some of the water. "Is your wound bothering you much?" she asked.

"I'm getting used to it." The wound was a dull fire spreading out from his shoulder, but with the bullet still lodged beneath the skin, he knew it would only get worse. The pain relievers, like the energy bar, might keep him going long enough to reach safety.

He dumped the rest of the first aid kit and the water bottle into the blankets and knotted them into a bundle he could carry on his back. "Do you really think we're going to need those?" Erin asked.

"I hope not, but I'd rather not get caught out with nothing. Besides, anything we take is something Duane's men can't use."

"I don't suppose you have a knife?"

"No, why?"

"We could slash the tires."

"I used nail scissors to puncture the tire of the Hummer the two men who caught you in the woods were driving," Mark said. "That slowed them down enough for me to ambush them."

"I wish we hadn't left the ax back at the cabin."

"It doesn't matter. This Hummer is already out of gas, and unless they're carrying extra with them, it will take them a while to get it fueled up again."

"Right." She looked up and he followed her gaze toward the low bank of clouds moving in. "Looks like we're in for more snow," she said.

"We should have planned our escape for better weather." He started forward. "Come on. We'd better start walking."

BETWEEN THE FALLING snow and the need to hide each time they heard a vehicle approaching, Erin and Mark traveled at a snail's pace. With each step, Erin imagined the timer that controlled the bomb at her throat ticking off another second. Instead of moving toward safety, she felt as if she were traveling toward her own destruction.

Beside her, Mark's breath grew more labored, his face grayer. The lines around his eyes deepened in pain, and he wore the grim look of a man determined to hang on at all costs. "Let me at least take the pack," she said.

"No, I've got it," he said, but when she reached up to slip the knotted blanket from his shoulder he didn't resist. As she settled the makeshift pack across her back he lifted his head, alert. "Car coming."

They scuttled for the roadside, sliding down through the snow into the ditch and struggling up the other side to crouch in the damp grass and trees. The vehicle, a white Jeep, zipped by, the woman behind the wheel never glancing in their direction.

Erin let out a breath, her heartbeat slowing its frantic gallop. These wild dashes to safety every time a car passed were more exhausting than the walking itself.

"Let's go," Mark said. He started up the slope and reached back to offer her his hand. But before she could take it, the rock gave way beneath him, sending him hurtling back toward her in a spray of loose gravel and mud.

She tried to catch him, but he slid past her

and landed hard on his injured shoulder, a sharp cry of pain piercing the air.

"Oh no! Are you okay?" She hurried to his side and tried to help him sit up.

He groaned and curled away from her. "Give me…a minute," he managed to say through clenched teeth.

She stared in horror as bright red blood blossomed at the shoulder of his coat. Had he torn open the wound again? Or worse, driven the bullet deeper? "Let me see," she said, and tried to push aside the fabric of his coat.

"Leave it." He grabbed her hand and held it. "There's nothing you can do. I'll be all right in a minute."

She wanted to argue with him, but he was right—what could she do? She wasn't a surgeon who could remove the bullet, or a nurse who could administer medication to dull the pain or fight off infection. All she could do was crouch beside him in the snowy ditch and wait for the tension to ease from his face, and for him to tell her he was ready to travel again.

The hum of tires on the wet road drew her attention and she peered through the underbrush at the burnt-orange Volkswagen bus trundling up the road toward them. She couldn't imagine Duane or one of his cohorts ever being caught in such a vehicle. When it was close enough for her to make out the Coexist and *Namaste* stickers on the front bumper, she was certain this driver, at least, had nothing to do with her malicious stepfather.

She rose and scrambled up the ditch embankment.

"Erin! What are you doing?" Mark called.

She ignored him and lifted a hand to flag down the bus. To her surprise and delight, the vehicle slowed with a screech of brakes and stopped several yards ahead of her on the shoulder of the road. The driver rolled down his window and looked back at her. White hair streamed from beneath a bright blue knit beany, the thin strands wafting in the breeze. "Are you okay, miss?" he asked.

"My friend and I were out, uh, hiking," she said, struggling to come up with a plausible story on the fly. "He fell and injured his shoulder and we need a ride to the nearest town for help."

The furrows on the man's forehead deepened. "Where were you hiking?" he asked.

"I don't remember the name," she said. "We're not from around here. We got lost and wandered pretty far off the trail. If you hadn't stopped, I don't know what we would have done. Will you give us a ride?"

"Sure I will." He climbed out of the cab and looked toward the ditch. "Is your friend down there?"

"I'll get him," she said. "Wait here a minute." She scooted back down into the ditch and into the trees.

"What are you doing?" Mark whispered when she reached him.

"I just saved us walking fourteen miles or however far it is." She slid her arm under his uninjured shoulder and helped him into a sitting position. "We'll need to leave the guns and everything else behind," she whispered.

"I don't like leaving the guns," he said.

"I told this guy we're hikers who got lost. If we show up with automatic weapons when we don't even have a real backpack, he'll know something is off."

Mark grimaced, but whether in pain or disagreement, she couldn't tell. "All right," he said, and started up the slope.

The driver was still waiting when Erin and Mark reached the road. Eyeing Mark, he let out a low whistle. "That looks like a pretty bad fall you took," he said.

"I'll be fine once we get to a town," Mark

answered, moving past the man to the open side door of the van.

"Dolorosa doesn't have a hospital," the driver said. "I think they have a little medical clinic, but I don't know the hours, or if they're set up to treat anything very serious."

"We just need to get to someplace we can call my brother." Mark rested his head on the back of the seat, eyes closed, then he sat up, suddenly more alert. "Do you have a cell phone we can use to make the call?" he asked.

The man slammed the van door shut, then climbed into the driver's seat. "I don't have one," he said. "I figure if I want to talk to anyone or anyone wants to talk to me, they can wait until I'm home." His eyes met Erin's in the rearview mirror. "Don't you have a cell phone? I thought all you young people couldn't live without the dang things."

"I left mine at home and Mark lost his when he fell," she said.

Mark looked impressed. Who knew she had such a talent for creative lying?

"There's a store in Dolorosa," the driver said. "They probably have a phone you can use." He pulled onto the road once more.

"How far is it to Dolorosa?" Erin asked.

"Another forty minutes or so," he said.

"Can't go too fast on these mountain roads." He laughed, a sound like wind escaping from leaky bellows. "Least ways, Sheila here won't go too fast on these uphill climbs."

"Sheila?" Erin didn't try to hide her confusion.

"My ride." Their chauffeur patted the cracked dashboard. "I bought her off an Australian guy, so the name seemed appropriate. My name's Gaither," he said.

"I'm Erin and this is Mark," she said. Now that they were off their feet and on their way to safety, she felt a little dazed.

"How big of a town is Dolorosa?" Mark asked.

"Oh, it's pretty small," Gaither said. "There's a few churches and stores and such, but nothing I'd call a tourist attraction or anything. The closest they have to that is the Pioneer Cemetery."

"What's that?" Erin asked.

"It's one of the oldest cemeteries in this part of the state," Gaither said. "People who are interested in genealogy or history, or who want to see the old markers, come to visit it, but that's about it. We get hikers and kayakers in the summer, and a few snowshoers and cross-country skiers in winter, but mostly Dolorosa is a pretty sleepy place."

Not a town likely to have a resident explosives expert, she thought, rubbing absently at the collar.

"What's with that thing around your neck?" Gaither asked.

She reached up to finger the collar, then jerked her hand away. She couldn't very well tell the old guy she was wearing a bomb, but any other explanation escaped her.

"It's the latest fashion." Mark's voice, so calm and reasonable, broke the awkward silence.

"What's with the flashing numbers?" Gaither asked.

"You've seen those fitness bracelets everyone wears these days?" Mark asked.

"Yeah. My daughter has one. I told her I don't see the point in counting your steps every day, but she said what she always says—that I'm too old-fashioned and out of touch." He snorted.

"This is sort of the same idea." Mark sat up, clearly warming to his subject. "But instead of counting steps, it counts down minutes and hours until you reset your fitness goals."

Erin fought the urge to pinch him or tell him to shut up. A fitness necklace? Did he really think anyone would fall for that story?

Gaither nodded. "My daughter would love that one. She likes everybody to think she's fit, even if she isn't." He glanced at Erin. "It don't look all that comfortable, though."

"Oh, you get used to it," she said airily.

Mark opened his mouth as if to elaborate, but shut it when she sent him a warning look.

"Thanks again for giving us a ride," she said. "Do you live around here?"

"I got me a place above Dolorosa, by the river," he said. "It's a yurt, with a woodstove and solar electric. Real cozy place. It suits me and Betty just fine."

"Betty? Is that another vehicle? Or a pet?"

He let out another wheezing laugh. "My old lady," he said. "She'd be with me today, but she's busy canning the last of the tomatoes from our greenhouse. She sent me to Dolorosa for more canning jars and a few other supplies."

Erin glanced to the back of the van, at the collection of cloth grocery bags, and tried to ignore her grumbling stomach.

"We heard on the news before we left for our

hike about that madman who's threatening to set off a nuclear bomb," Mark said. "Do you know any more about that?"

"I stopped listening to the news years ago," Gaither said. "The press always distorts everything and it's all just depressing anyway."

"So you haven't heard about this terrorist, Duane Braeswood, who says he has a nuclear bomb?" Mark asked. "He says he's going to set it off if the government doesn't meet his demands."

"How would one guy get hold of the technology to make a nuclear bomb?" Gaither asked. "It's been a while since I was in college, but from what I remember, it takes more than a couple of pounds of plutonium and some fuses to do that kind of thing."

Mark's eyes met Erin's. "Maybe he persuaded a nuclear physicist to work for him," he said.

Gaither shook his head. "What a waste of an intellect. Why is this guy making these threats anyway?"

"Apparently, the leader of this terrorist group thinks the only way to fix the country is to destroy it," Erin said.

"That's like burning down the forest to get rid of a little patch of poison ivy," Gaither said.

"Do you have a radio we could turn on, see if there's any news?" Mark asked.

Gaither shook his head. "When I bought Sheila, she had an eight-track tape player," he said. "But I pulled that out a long time ago." He patted a rectangular hole on the dash. "I prefer listening to my own thoughts."

Erin sagged back against the seat. Her own thoughts were in too much turmoil to make good company.

"Don't get me wrong," Gaither said. "I hope they catch these crazies, but I don't see how me fretting over the matter will help anyone."

"I suppose you're right," she said. But she wished they could find out more, if only to see if they fit into the puzzle anywhere. Had Duane planned this ultimatum all along, or had something she or Mark had done triggered this outburst?

"Where are you two from?" Gaither asked.

"Denver," Mark said.

"Idaho," Erin said.

"Denver and Idaho. So you just met up here for a little vacation?"

"Yes," she said, and tried for a bright smile.

Gaither raked his hand over his chin, which bristled with several days' growth of beard. "Don't take this wrong," he said. "But if you're going to go hiking here in the mountains, you ought to be a little better prepared. You need good packs and emergency supplies and water. A map and a compass come in handy, too."

Mark had compressed his lips into a thin line. Maybe he was thinking about how he had set out with all those things when he had left home on his last hiking trip, a year ago. "We'll remember that next time," he said.

Erin settled back into the seat and closed her eyes. The warmth of the van and the hum of the highway lulled her to sleep. She woke with a start when the van stopped.

"We're in Dolorosa," Gaither announced. He climbed out and opened the van's side door. He peered in at them and nodded. "You're looking a lot better, Mister. I was a little worried when I first saw you, but I guess you'll make it now."

"I'll be fine." Mark climbed out after Erin and offered the older man his hand. "Thank you."

Gaither shook his hand. "Shorty will help you out." He slammed the van door. "I'd better be going. Betty needs those jars." He climbed back into the driver's seat and, with a wave, puttered away.

Chapter Thirteen

Erin took a deep breath and looked at Mark. "I guess we'd better go inside and get this over with," she said.

"Yeah." He took her arm. "Maybe I should let you do the talking. You have quite the talent for spinning tales."

"I guess I do my best work under pressure." She tried for a smile, but her lips wobbled dangerously.

Mark hugged her close. "Hang on a little longer," he said soothingly. "We're almost there."

The Dolorosa Country Store looked considerably more prosperous than McCarty's. New gas pumps gleamed on concrete islands out front, and brightly colored posters on the double glass doors leading inside advertised tobacco products, energy drinks and lottery tickets. Erin searched for a newspaper box amid the gallons of washer fluid and cases of soda stacked in pyramids on either side of the door, but saw none.

Cowbells jangled as Mark pulled open the door. The smells of fresh coffee and frying chicken made Erin stagger and her mouth water to the point she was afraid she might start drooling. She clung to Mark's arm, heart pounding as they approached the middle-aged woman behind the front counter.

"Excuse me," Mark began.

The woman didn't look up from the invoice she was studying.

"Excuse me." Mark spoke louder this time.

She raised her head to stare at him with pale brown eyes behind black-rimmed glasses, but said nothing.

"Could we please use your phone?" Mark asked. "We've been hiking and got lost. The man who gave us a ride here said you would have a phone we could use to call for help."

"Pay phone's out front." She pointed a long, orange-tipped nail toward the door.

Mark looked pained. "I fell hiking and hurt my shoulder. I lost my wallet with all our money in it."

The woman's expression didn't change.

"Please, we just need to make one phone call," Erin said.

The clerk's eyes shifted to meet hers. "If I gave away stuff to every beggar that wandered in here asking, I'd go broke inside of a month," she said.

Erin took a step forward. She wasn't sure what she intended to do, though her first impulse was to slap the smug look off the woman's face. Her second impulse was to burst into angry tears, but she doubted that would draw this woman's sympathy.

Mark put a restraining hand on her arm. "Is there someplace else in town that might have a phone we could use?" he asked. "Or is there a sheriff's office or a police department?"

The woman snorted. "You think the cops will lend you a quarter for the phone?"

It was Mark's turn to deliver the silent treatment.

"We got a deputy who swings through here every once in a while," she said. "But we don't get a lot of crime around here, so he doesn't have cause to be here often. And knowing him, he's fresh out of quarters."

Erin was exhausted, half-starved, frightened and angry and fed up. "Why can't you just be a decent human being and help us?" she raged.

"All we're asking is to borrow your phone for five minutes to make one lousy phone call. We'll even call collect. Then you never have to look at us again."

The woman's eyes narrowed. "I pay for that phone, and if you want to use it, you have to pay for the privilege."

"Fine." Erin unhooked the gold hoop from one ear and laid it on the counter. "That's fourteen karat gold. You can sell it in any jewelry store for way more than your phone bill."

The woman's hand shot out and she swept the earring off the counter, then reached under and pulled out an old-fashioned black plastic corded phone. "Five minutes," she said, and turned away.

Mark seized the phone and wiped his free hand on his jeans. He punched in his brother's number, then leaned toward Erin, so that she could listen with him. The phone buzzed three time. Four times. Erin suppressed a moan. What if they had gone through all this and Mark's brother didn't answer his phone?

"Luke Renfro." The clipped voice on the other end of the line was so like Mark's that Erin might have imagined the man beside her was speaking.

"Luke." The word came out hoarse, more of

a croak than speech. Mark cleared his throat and tried again. "Luke, it's Mark," he said.

The man on the other end of the line was silent so long Erin worried he had hung up. "This better not be a joke," he said.

"It isn't a joke. It's really me," Mark said. "I need your help, Luke. I'm in a little store in a place called Dolorosa, Colorado. It's in the mountains. Duane Braeswood and his men kidnapped me and they've been holding me hostage. I managed to get away a couple of days ago, but they're looking for me."

"Give me your number so I can call you back." Erin heard scrabbling noises, as if he was searching for a piece of paper.

"It's the phone for the Dolorosa Country Store," Mark said. "I don't know the number. The woman behind the counter let us use it to make one call. Please, send someone to get us right away."

"Us?"

"I have Erin Daniels with me. Braeswood kidnapped her, too. She's his stepdaughter."

"We know who Ms. Daniels is."

Erin blinked. The FBI knew her? Did they suspect she was in league with Duane? Her stomach flipped at the idea.

"She helped me escape," Mark said.

"Is there somewhere safe you can wait for me?" Luke asked. "It may be a while before I can get to you. I don't know if you've heard about the trouble Duane Braeswood has been causing us, but we've got every available agent working overtime on this."

"I heard part of a news story," Mark said. He glanced toward the clerk, who was shuffling her stack of invoices, but clearly listening. "I have some information that can help you with that, but you need to get to us as soon as possible. We're not safe. And there's something else."

"What else?" Luke asked. "Are you hurt?"

"I have a gunshot wound that probably needs attention, but that's not the biggest problem. Before we got away from him, Duane Braeswood wired a bomb to Erin." He glanced at the display on her collar. "It's set to go off in a little over twelve hours."

"A bomb! You didn't say anything about a bomb." The clerk snatched the phone from Mark's hand. She stared at them, wild-eyed. "I don't know what kind of crazy you are, but you get out of here right this minute."

"Or what?" Mark snapped. "You'll call the sheriff? Well, go ahead. He's just the man I'd like to see."

"I won't waste my time with the sheriff." The woman slammed down the phone, reached under the counter and pulled out a sawed-off shotgun. "Get out. Now!"

Mark raised his hands and backed toward the door. Erin hurried after him. When they were outside, he wrapped his arm around her and they hurried across the road, to a treeless gravel lot where two tractor-trailer rigs and a rusting bulldozer were parked. "That woman is as nasty and crazy as Duane," Erin said when they were out of sight, and hopefully out of range, of the clerk.

"She's definitely not a people person." Mark leaned back against the bulldozer.

The snow had stopped but the clouds remained, and the air was icy and heavy with moisture. Erin rubbed her shoulders. "I wish I had one of those blankets now," she said.

Mark held out his arms. "Come here," he said.

She came to him and let him wrap his arms around her. The solid feel of him made her feel safer and warmer. "Will your brother send help?" she asked.

"He will." Mark rested his chin atop her head. "He may not be able to come himself, but he'll know people in the Bureau's Denver office, or maybe an office even closer to this part of the state. He'll send someone." He hoped the Bureau's desire to find out everything Mark and Erin knew about Duane would speed them along.

"Why do you think Luke said he knows me?" she asked. "You don't think they believe I'm part of Duane's horrible organization, do you?"

"They probably have profiles on any family members of known terrorists," Mark said. "That doesn't mean they think you're guilty of anything. But they'll want to find out everything we know about Duane. Maybe our information will help them to track him down and stop him."

"When they find Duane, what will happen to my mother?" Erin had never dared voice this question before. Maybe she hadn't believed anyone, before Mark, would understand her concern.

"I don't know the law," he said. "She might have to go to jail as an accessory, if they believe she has helped him or lied to protect him."

Erin nodded, the fabric of his shirt shifting beneath her cheek with the movement. "I tell myself she's an adult. She made this choice.

But I can't believe she ever condoned the bad things Duane has done. She did what she did out of some misguided idea of love."

"Maybe the prosecutors will take that into account. You can speak on her behalf."

"At least in jail she'll be safe from Duane," Erin said.

The front door of the store opened and the clerk stepped out and looked around. Mark and Erin shrank farther into the shadows of the machinery. "Maybe she did call the sheriff," Erin said.

"I hope she did," Mark said. "At least in his custody we'll be safe."

"Unless Duane has paid off local officials."

"Do you really think he does that?"

"I've learned not to underestimate anything he will do," she said. "All his money and followers have given him an outsize ambition and an overly positive opinion of himself to go with it." She closed her eyes and snuggled against Mark. "I just want to have a bath, eat a good meal and get a good night's sleep. Not necessarily in that order." She wanted to do all those things with him. And when they woke, she wanted to make love to him slowly and thoroughly, with no worries about being interrupted, and with a whole box of condoms at their disposal.

Whether he wanted the same thing she couldn't tell, and she was afraid to ask.

A white panel van pulled up to the store and a man wearing khakis and a black leather jacket got out and went inside. Less than a minute later he came out, got in the van again and backed out of the parking lot.

Erin closed her eyes again, and was wondering if it was possible to sleep standing up when she felt Mark stiffen. She opened her eyes and pulled away from him. "What's wrong?"

"That van is headed this way." He nodded toward the road, where the van was already turning into the lot. The driver drove slowly until he was almost even with them and stopped, the van blocking their view of the road. The driver's window rolled down and a middle-aged man with a softly lined faced studied them. "Rosalie tells me you folks need some help," he said, in a voice that hinted at origins in the South.

Mark stepped in front of Erin, shielding her with his body. "Thanks, but someone is on the way to help us," he said.

The metallic sound of the slide of a pistol being pulled back sent ice through Erin's veins.

She remained frozen in place as the muzzle of the weapon appeared in the window of the van. "Y'all want to come along quietly and there won't be any trouble," the driver said.

Chapter Fourteen

Mark wanted to howl in rage or lash out in fury, but such temper would be foolish in the face of the gun. He glanced toward the store across the street, but the parking lot and doorway were vacant. Behind him, Erin stood so close her trembling moved through him. She had been so strong, had been through so much. To have it all end now when they had just found each other engulfed him in a dragging sadness. "How did you find us?" he asked.

The man with the gun didn't quite smile. "We have our ways." He motioned toward the back of the van. "Get in."

"Where are you taking us?" Erin asked, as the door opened and a larger man dressed in jeans and a flannel hunting jacket climbed out and took hold of her wrist.

"Mr. Braeswood wants to see you," the driver said.

They climbed into the van, where a third man waited. Outnumbered this way, Mark and Erin would have no chance of overpowering their enemies. Duane might have underestimated them before, but not now.

Mark had thought their captors might take them back to the cabin, or even into Denver. Instead, the van cruised slowly down Dolorosa's main street, then stopped in front of a modest house, the kind that might be rented out to vacationing skiers in winter or fishermen in summer. A tattered wreath hung on the front door, the faded red ribbon fluttering in the breeze.

The front door opened and the driver waited in the van while the two guards escorted Erin and Mark into the house at gunpoint. The door slammed behind them, the sound echoing in the darkened room, which was devoid of furniture.

"Professor Renfro."

Mark turned toward the sound in time to see a wheelchair glide through a doorway to the right, flanked by two more guards. Mark took a step toward them and one of the guards pointed a rifle at him. Duane's eyes burned the intense blue of a Bunsen burner. "Don't let my injuries fool you," he said. "At my word any one of my men would kill for me, though I hope it won't come to that."

Mark waited. Better to say nothing and see if he could figure out what Braeswood wanted from them.

"I examined that trunk you tried to foist off on my men," Duane continued, the hiss and click of the oxygen tank punctuating his words. "Very clever."

"It's not real," Mark said. "You can't blow up anything with it."

Duane's head bobbed up and down, the oxygen tube jerking with each movement. "Not in the state it was in when you left it, but I have many resources at my disposal."

"You couldn't have armed that thing," Mark said. "It's impossible."

"Maybe it is. Or maybe it isn't. The Feds can't risk the chance that I'm telling the truth, so they'll give in to my demands." His lips twisted in a distorted smile. "So you see, even though you didn't do the job I wanted, you did enough to help carry out my goals."

"What are your demands?" Erin asked.

Duane shifted cold eyes to her. "I'm demanding the immediate resignation of the president and his cabinet. I will replace them with persons handpicked for the job—men who share my vision for steering the country on the correct course once more."

"You won't get away with this," Mark said. "They'll never believe the bomb is real. It's impossible."

"They'll believe me when I tell them the esteemed nuclear physicist Mark Renfro created the device for me. I have pictures of you working in your secluded lab to show them. Your fingerprints are on the device. Your DNA is in it, in a matter of speaking. When they learn such a reputable scientist is behind the project, they'll have no choice but to believe."

"No!" Mark's vision misted with rage. "I had nothing to do with the kind of evil you're perpetrating."

"But now your name will be associated with it forever," Duane said. "When people think of you in the future, they'll remember a terrorist. Your daughter will be ashamed to tell anyone that you were her father."

Mark lunged toward the man in the wheelchair, but before he had moved six inches he was knocked to the floor by one of the bodyguards. He lay there, lip bleeding, staring up at Duane. He had thought he could never despise anyone more than he had despised this man, but Duane had found a way to increase his hatred. "I hope you burn in hell," Mark said. "If I ever find a way, I'll send you there myself."

"There is a way you could save your reputation," Duane said. "Or rather, avoid it being tarnished in the press."

"What is it?" Mark hated how quickly he took Duane's bait, but thoughts of his daughter growing up with her reputation tarnished because she shared his name—possibly even growing to hate him because of it—drove him.

"You were clever enough that I can see you are very close to creating the weapon I'm looking for," Duane said. "A few more weeks, maybe months, and you would have built a working nuclear weapon. I want you to come back to a new lab I'll build for you and finish the job."

"Never!" Mark said. "I won't be any part of that kind of evil."

Duane made a wheezing sound that might have been a chuckle. "Not interested?" He subsided into a fit of coughing. One of the guards stepped toward him, but Duane waved him away. When the coughing ceased, he wiped a tear from his eye and grinned at Mark. "Maybe I can change your mind about that."

He turned to look across the room. The door opened and a little girl edged into the room. Light brown curls formed a halo around her face and thick dark lashes framed sky-blue eyes. She clutched a stuffed elephant to her chest and looked around, cheeks flushed, lips trembling. At last her gaze came to rest on Mark. "Daddy?" she whispered.

ERIN STARED AT the girl, then the man. Mark had struggled to his feet, but now all the color drained from his face. He swayed, then sank to his knees. "Mandy," he sobbed.

The little girl ran to him and threw her arms around him. He held her tightly against him and buried his face in her hair, tears streaming down his cheeks. Erin wiped tears from her own eyes and sniffed.

"A touching scene, isn't it?"

She stiffened, and turned to find that Duane had glided his chair alongside her. "That might have been you and I under different circumstances."

"That could never have been you and me."

"Only because you weren't willing to listen to the wisdom I had to share. You always insisted on going your own way."

"Because your way is crazy," she said. "You

enjoy torturing and manipulating people for your own twisted ends. Do you know how sick that is?"

His expression hardened. "It's very easy for people to dismiss things they don't understand as madness," he said. "Despite what you wish to believe, it isn't mental illness that drives me, but a clear determination to do whatever is necessary to make this country great once more. The reason we have fallen so far from our ideals is that so few people are willing to do what is necessary to restore greatness. As the good book reminds us, we must separate the wheat from the chaff, and the sheep from the goats."

"Why do you get to decide the definition of greatness?" she asked.

"Again, because I am one of the few people with the ability to see things as they should be, and the courage to take action." He gave her a coy smile. "Did you like the little gift I gave you?"

"What gift? I don't want any gifts from you."

"The necklace, of course. Very haute couture, don't you think? I even went to the trouble to gold plate it, in case you suffer from an allergy to base metals."

"What do you think it's going to do to my mother if you blow me up?" Erin asked, resisting the urge to tug at the neckband.

"When she sees what I'm willing to do to those who cross me, Helen will never think of leaving me again."

The coldness in his eyes made her shiver. But she forced herself to meet his gaze. "Let Mark and his daughter go," she said. "Find another scientist to make your bomb—one who actually believes in your cause."

"So, you've developed feelings for my scientist," he said. "And here I was beginning to think you were incapable of normal womanly affection. A female eunuch, as it were."

"You don't know anything about me," she said.

"I know everything about you." His voice grew harsher. "You may have thought you were out of my reach, but I have made it my business to know what you were up to at all times. Not many women your age have never had a successful relationship with a man—or a woman."

"You're the reason I never had a relationship," she said. "I never wanted to put anyone else in danger from you."

He laughed. "And now you've gone and

fallen for the professor who is, after all, already under my control."

"Let him go," she said again, not caring if he laughed at her affections. If she had to die, at least she could know she had saved Mark and his little girl.

"Forget about me. Let Erin go."

She and Duane turned to find that Mark had risen, Mandy in his arms. The little girl had her head on his chest, her arms around his neck, but she watched the others with wary eyes.

"Why should I let her go?" Duane asked. "If she stays you can continue your touching little romance—as long as it doesn't interfere with your work."

"Let her go," Mark said. He unwrapped his daughter's arms from around him and set her on the ground. "She can take Mandy with her. I'll do whatever you want as long as you let the two of them go free."

"No, Mark." Erin's words were full of anguish as she looked at him. It hurt to look at her, to think about what they might have had if Duane hadn't interfered.

He nudged Mandy toward her. "Go to Erin," he said. "She'll look after you."

His daughter gazed up at him, her eyes so

like her mother's he felt a stab of grief—not the sharp, raw longing to be with his wife again, but the dull ache of acknowledgment that their time had passed. He had room in his heart for a new love now, but Duane was determined to take that from him, as well.

"I want to stay with you, Daddy," Mandy said.

"I know, sweetheart. I want to stay with you, too." Mark patted her shoulder. "But more than that, I want you to be safe." He nudged her again and, head down, she walked to Erin's side. She reached up and slipped her hand into Erin's, and the young woman gave her a wobbly, wet-eyed smile.

Mark forced his gaze away from them, to the broken man in the wheelchair. Rage clawed at the back of his throat as he met Duane's smug grin. How had so many people allowed Duane Braeswood's money and power to bulldoze over everything that was right and just? Why didn't more people fight back? Why hadn't *he* fought back more when Duane first kidnapped him? He had had so much to fight for, yet he had allowed this little man to take everything from him, even his dignity.

"Promise me you'll let Erin and Mandy go

and I'll build you all the bombs you want," Mark said.

"But I only need one," Duane said. "And when it's done, you'll have outlived your usefulness to me and I'll have to kill you."

Mark nodded. Hearing the words out loud shook him, though Duane wasn't telling him anything he hadn't already known. But he didn't intend to give the madman a chance to end his life. Or to make use of any bomb he might build.

"Mark, don't do this," Erin protested.

"Take them into the next room," Duane said, and one of the guards took hold of Erin's arm. A second guard scooped up Mandy.

"Let go of me, you bully!" The little girl kicked and clawed at the man who held her. "Put me down." When the guard ignored her, she leaned over and bit his ear, hard. Yowling, he punched the side of her head.

Mark didn't remember lunging for Braeswood. He didn't remember upending the wheelchair and pinning the frail body to the floor. When he came to his senses again he had one knee planted on the older man's chest, his hands around his throat, the oxygen cannula ripped away. Duane stared up at him, eyes bulging as Mark squeezed.

"Let him go." The barrel of the gun was hard and cold, pressed against the back of Mark's head.

"Go ahead and shoot," Mark said. "I'll snap his neck first." He could feel Duane's pulse jumping beneath his fingers, could hear him fighting for breath.

"Don't…shoot," Duane wheezed.

The man with the gun backed away and Mark relaxed his grip on Duane's throat a little, though he kept his knee planted in his chest and his eyes locked to his enemy's. "Who has the power now?" he asked.

Hate edged out fear in Duane's eyes. "What… are you going…to do?" he gasped.

Good question. Mark hadn't exactly formulated a plan. He'd acted on instinct when the guard had gone after his little girl. "Let Megan and Erin go," he said. "Now."

"Do it," Duane said.

Mark heard movement behind him, then Erin was standing beside him, Mandy in her arms. "Mark…" she began.

"Take Mandy outside and wait," he said. "I'll be out in a minute."

He waited until the door closed behind her, then he grabbed Duane by the shoulders and hauled him upright. The once-powerful man weighed little more than a child, and his legs dangled uselessly, incapable of supporting him. "I need my chair," he said. "My oxygen."

"I prefer you helpless." Holding Duane tight to his chest, Mark turned to the closest guard. "Give me your gun," he said, and held out his good hand.

The man glowered at Mark, who responded by squeezing Duane tighter. "Give it to him!" Duane ordered.

Reluctantly, the man handed over the large pistol he had tucked in his belt.

"And your keys," Mark said.

The man passed him the keys. "Which vehicle do these go with?" Mark asked.

"Black Jeep parked on the side."

Mark took a firmer grip on Duane. "All right, Duane. Are you ready to go for a ride?"

"You'll never…get away…with this," Duane huffed.

"Maybe you haven't figured out yet that I'm a man who has nothing to lose." He held the pistol on the three guards and dragged Duane toward the door.

Once outside, he moved to where Erin and Mandy waited. He pressed the keys into Erin's hand. "Take Mandy with you in the Jeep parked on the side of the house. Get out of here. Don't stop until you get to a good-sized town. Do you still have Luke's number?"

She nodded.

"Good. When you get to a safe place, call Luke and let him know where you are."

"What are you going to do?" she asked.

"I'm leaving, too. Duane is my ticket out of here."

"Daddy, don't leave me," Mandy said.

He focused attention on his little girl. "I'm only leaving you for a little bit," he said. "I'll come get you soon and then I promise I'll never leave you again." He hoped he was telling the truth. "Right now, I want you to go with Erin. She'll take good care of you."

She nodded solemnly and looked up at Erin.

"I don't like leaving you," Erin said. "We should all go together."

He shook his head. "It's safer for you this way."

"What are you going to do with him?" She nodded to Duane.

"I don't know yet." He tightened his grip on the older man. "Though I can think of a few things I'd like to do. I'd like to make him suffer the way he's made all of us suffer."

"If you…kill me…you'll have…a legion

after you," Duane said. "They won't rest…
until…they avenge me."

Mark wondered if Duane was right. Would
he stop Duane, only to have to contend with
an even larger and more menacing threat in his
wake—a tribe of followers fired up for battle
by the image of a martyr?

Mark didn't have time to worry about that
now. He had to make sure Erin and Mandy got
away, before any more of Duane's followers
showed up. "Go!" he ordered her. "I'll catch
up with you as soon as I can."

Chapter Fifteen

Erin took Mandy's hand and led her around the side of the house to the Jeep. The girl climbed into the backseat and Erin buckled her in. "Are you okay?" she asked.

Mandy shrugged and looked away. Erin resisted the urge to gather her up in a hug. The poor girl had been passed around among so many people she probably resisted getting close to anyone anymore. Erin knew what that was like.

Driving away from Mark was one of the most difficult things she had ever done, but she knew keeping Mandy safe was more important than what either of them wanted. She glanced in the rearview mirror as she pulled onto the street and saw him leading Duane toward the white van.

"Where is Daddy going?" Mandy asked.

"Not too far, I don't think," Erin said. "Your uncle Luke is coming to get him soon."

"I like Uncle Luke," Mandy said. "And I like his girlfriend, Morgan, too. They're going to be married soon and I get to be in the wedding."

"Oh?" She watched in the rearview mirror as the van backed out of the driveway and started down the street. How was Luke going to find his brother if they got too far out of town? Somebody needed to keep track of him and Duane. And what about Duane's driver? Maybe a threat to Duane would be enough to keep him in line, but what if he decided to play the hero? How would Mark handle it with his attention divided between Duane and the driver?

She drove to the corner, then made a U-turn in the street. "Are we going after them?" Mandy asked.

"We're just going to make sure they're okay," Erin said.

"That's a very bad man with Daddy," Mandy said. "He took me from my aunt Claire and brought me here."

"When was this?" Erin asked.

"Yesterday. I had to spend the night locked

in the back of that white van. They gave me Toaster Strudel for dinner."

A chill ran through Erin, and she gripped the steering wheel hard to control the sudden shaking in her hands. "Did those men hurt you?" she asked.

"I have a bruise on my arm where one of them grabbed me, but he has a bigger bruise on his leg where I kicked him back. After that the old guy in the wheelchair told him to leave me alone." She paused, then added, "Mostly, I was just scared and lonely."

Erin had been scared and lonely a lot in the past months and years. Duane had managed to isolate her even when he hadn't physically held her in custody. "I won't let them get to you again," she said, and vowed to keep that promise.

"Look at that funny car." Mandy leaned forward against her seat belt and pointed out the front windshield at the burnt-orange VW van puttering along in front of them.

Erin almost smiled. What was Gaither still doing in town? They made an odd parade—the white van, the VW and the Jeep, never driving over twenty-five miles an hour through the gravel streets. The van pulled into a small park, where picnic tables and a baseball backstop were visible in the distance. Gaither stopped, too, positioning his bus crookedly across the entrance to the park. Erin pulled in across the street, and left the Jeep's motor running.

"What is that man doing?" Mandy asked.

Erin wondered the same thing as Gaither climbed out of the VW. He watched the van for a few moments, then started toward it. Erin had a sudden, horrible vision of the old man being injured in a firefight, or taken hostage by Duane. She rolled down her window. "Gaither!" she called. "What are you doing here?"

He reversed course and crossed the street to them. "Hello, Erin," he said, his gaze taking in the Jeep and the girl in the backseat. "Is that your friend Mark in the van over there?"

"Yes." She tried for a smile that conveyed innocence. "What brings you back to town so soon?"

The old man rubbed his chin. "Well, I got to thinking after I dropped you off at the store. I remembered Rosalie was working today, not Shorty, and she isn't a woman overly blessed with the milk of human kindness, you might say. My conscience started bothering me, so I swung back by to check on you. Rosalie told me your friend in a white van picked you up.

That struck me as kind of odd. I knew he must have been close, to reach you that quick, but you hadn't said anything about him being a local, though maybe I misunderstood." He tugged at one ear. "My hearing isn't what it used to be."

"But when you saw the white van you decided to follow it," Erin said.

"Something like that." He glanced over his shoulder at the vehicle. No one had emerged from it. "Right now I'm trying to figure out how you two went from no transportation at all to having two new-looking rides." His gaze shifted to the backseat once more. "And a little girl."

Erin sighed. "It's a really long story."

"We're waiting for my uncle to get here," Mandy said.

"Does he live around here?" Gaither asked.

"No. He lives in Durango. He works for the FBI."

Time to cut this off before Mandy started spilling their life histories. The less the old man knew about Duane and his organization, the safer he would be. "Gaither, I appreciate all the help you've given us, but we're fine," she said. "Really."

"I can't say I've had a lot of experience,"

he said. "But I didn't think the FBI showed up unless there was trouble. Are you in some kind of trouble?"

"We'll be fine once Mark's brother gets here." Erin tried to sound confident. "But I think you should leave, just in case there is trouble."

"Well, I don't know." He shifted his gaze toward the van. "This a lot more interesting than watching Betty can tomatoes."

"Please go," Erin pleaded.

At that moment the door to the van burst open and Duane Braeswood fell out. Mark tumbled after him, and the two rolled around on the ground, grappling for the pistol, each fighting for a firm grip on the weapon as it waved about. The driver jumped out of the van also, and pulled a gun, but the two wrestled too furiously for him to get a clear shot.

"Why am I beginning to think the two of you aren't ordinary hikers?" Gaither asked in a conversational tone.

"That's my daddy with a very bad man," Mandy said. "He kidnapped my daddy and then he kidnapped me to try to make Daddy do some very bad things."

Gaither looked at Erin, his eyebrows raised in question. She sighed. "That about sums it up," she said. She watched the two men roll around on the ground, the driver hovering over them. "I don't suppose you have a gun on you?"

"I don't believe in them any more than I do cell phones," he said.

Of course he didn't. "Right now a cell phone and a gun would come in handy," she said. She could call Luke Renfro on the phone and tell him to hurry up, and use the gun to hold off the driver.

"Looks to me like your friend is getting the better of the old guy," Gaither said.

Luke straddled Duane, one hand wrapped around the grip of the pistol. The driver moved in closer. "Great. As long as the driver doesn't shoot him," Erin said.

"I can take care of him," Gaither said.

She stared at him. "How are you going to do that?"

He stooped and picked up a fist-sized rock from the side of the road and hefted it in his palm. Then he pulled his arm back and hurled the stone, striking the driver in the head. The man slumped to the ground as if shot.

Erin gaped as Gaither brushed the dirt from his hands. "How did you do that?" she asked.

"I used to play minor league ball," he said.

"It's been a few decades, but I still stay in practice." His eyes met hers. "I said I didn't believe in guns, not that I didn't believe in being able to defend myself. Now I'll see if your friend needs any help."

He strode across the street, and together he and Mark tied up Duane and the guard and stowed them in the van. Erin started the Jeep and drove to meet them.

Mark walked to the driver's side window. "You were supposed to go far away from here, where you'd be safe," he said.

"Somebody has to keep an eye on you." Her gaze met his and she felt the shimmer of heat through her. He leaned closer and she parted her lips, willing him to kiss her. Later, when they were alone, she would tell him how much she loved him, but for now the kiss would be enough.

"Daddy, can I get out of the car now?"

Mandy's question brought Erin out of her lovesick daze. Mark opened the back door of the Jeep and gingerly pulled his daughter into his arms. Balancing her on his hip, he carried her over to Gaither, and the three of them fell into conversation.

Erin unbuckled her seat belt, but she didn't get out of the Jeep. She smoothed her hand along the steering wheel and fought to subdue a storm of emotions. Of course Mark belonged with his daughter now. The child needed him, and they both needed time to heal. Erin had been a pleasant distraction while the two of them had been thrown together, but now they were back to real life. In real life a distinguished scientist and single dad didn't have a romance with the stepdaughter of the man who had killed his wife, kidnapped him and his daughter, and generally made his life hell. Erin had been a fool to ever believe otherwise.

Brakes squealed as a trio of black SUVs came around the corner, sending up rooster tails of dust in their wake. The first vehicle skidded to a halt inches from the bumper of the Jeep and a handsome, dark-haired man wearing black trousers and a black quilted jacket jumped out. Luke Renfro looked enough like his brother that Erin might have momentarily mistaken them for one another in a crowd. The two men faced each other, the one freshly groomed in black tactical gear, the other bloodstained and weary, with shaggy hair and several days' growth of beard. They were like before and after photos of the same man. They stood immobile for a long while, staring, as if trying to convince themselves this moment was real.

"Hi, Uncle Luke." Mandy broke the spell. "Daddy's back."

Luke went to his brother and the two men embraced, the girl sandwiched between them. Luke drew back and looked into his brother's eyes. "I'm sure you have a hell of a story to tell," he said. "And I want to hear it all. But right now I'm just glad you're safe."

"Duane Braeswood and one of his men are tied up in the van," Mark said. "You'll want to check out the white house two streets over, where they were staying."

Luke turned and signaled to the vehicle that had parked behind him, and a trio of men in SWAT gear piled out and headed for the van. Then he gave a dispatcher the information about the house and told her to send a team in to check it out. "What can you tell us about this nuclear bomb Braeswood is threatening to set off?" he asked Mark.

"It's not real," Mark said. "It's a fake I made. But it's not armed."

"You made a terrorist a bomb?" The muscles of Luke's jaw tightened and Erin feared he might punch his brother.

"Braeswood killed Christy. He threatened

to kill Mandy. I had to at least pretend to cooperate with him. I stalled as long as I could, then, when he upped the pressure, I made a decoy bomb."

"So he thinks it's a real bomb," Luke said.

"He knows it's not real," Mark said. "But he's arrogant enough to believe you won't call his bluff."

"Maybe he found someone to turn your decoy into a real weapon," Luke said.

"There's no way he could have gotten the material to arm it," Mark said.

"Are you sure of that?" Luke's expression was grim.

"I'd bet my life on it."

"What about the lives of innocent people?"

"If you find the bomb you can prove to yourself that it's harmless," Erin said.

Luke shifted his gaze to Erin, then walked over to her, Mark and Mandy trailing after him. "Ms. Daniels?" Luke asked.

She released her grip on the steering wheel of the Jeep and rested her hands in her lap. "It's nice to meet you, Agent Renfro," she said. She managed a smile, but his attention was already focused on the collar around her neck. "Is that the bomb?" he asked. "On the phone,

Mark said something about you being wired with a bomb."

"Yes." She wet her lips. "At least, according to my stepfather it is."

Luke's eyes met hers again. "Do you know where Duane has hidden this nuclear weapon he's threatening to detonate?"

She shook her head. "No, but it's probably somewhere in Colorado. I don't think he's had time to move it anywhere else."

"We can't be sure of that," Mark said. "It's possible he shipped it to one of his followers in New York or DC or another major city. One thing in our favor, though. I don't know what he told you, but it's not a suitcase nuke. The decoy I built is in a big metal trunk. It's big enough people would notice it, and it's really heavy. It takes two strong men to move it."

Luke nodded and took out his phone. "I'll spread the word." He shifted his gaze to Mark. "Then we'll see about getting you to the hospital to have a look at that shoulder. Don't think I haven't noticed you favoring it."

"I can wait a little longer," Mark said. In the excitement of the last hour, he had almost forgotten the pain of the gunshot wound.

"Why are the numbers flashing on your necklace?" Mandy asked.

"Are they flashing?" Erin lowered the visor and craned her neck to see in the mirror. The display on the collar had changed from green to red and the numbers flashed with each changing second, a horrible pulse counting down her doom.

But it wasn't the flashing red numbers that shocked her as much as the time displayed. "This says... I've got less than an hour." She stared at Mark in horror.

"That's because no matter what you do to me, I'm still in charge!" Duane, held between two agents in black flak jackets and fatigues, screamed the words like curses. "You think you can stop me, but you never can."

The agents dragged him away to one of the SUVs, shoved him in the backseat and drove away. A second set of agents hauled away the van's driver.

"Where is your explosives expert?" Mark asked.

"He's on his way." Luke's voice was more clipped than ever, his expression strained.

"Where is he coming from?" Erin asked.

"From Denver." Luke refused to meet her gaze. Instead, he turned to his brother. "You told me we had more time."

"We did. Braeswood must have reset the timing mechanism."

Luke pulled a set of keys from his pocket and handed them to Mark. "You take Mandy and get out of here," he said. "There's a medical clinic a couple of streets over where you can get that arm checked out. I'll stay with Ms. Daniels."

"I'll stay with her," Mark said, and his words made Erin weak with relief.

"Your place is with your daughter," Luke said.

He bowed his head. Erin felt his struggle, but she knew Luke was right. "Go with Mandy," she said. "There's nothing you can do to help me anyway." It was her turn to look away, before he could see her sadness and longing for what might have been.

She listened to his footsteps walking away, then the sounds of the car door slamming and the engine starting. She bit the inside of her cheek to keep from crying out as he drove off. Even if she survived this ordeal, she doubted she would see him again. Oh, they might run into each other during a court trial, if it came to that, but he needed time to reconnect with his daughter and the rest of his family. She didn't fit into his plans.

"Sir, you'll have to leave now, too."

Erin realized Luke was speaking to Gaither, who had stood nearby and silently watched the whole drama unfold. She would have to be sure Luke knew the part the older man had played in saving them. Maybe he'd get a medal.

"What's going to happen to her?" Gaither asked.

"Someone will be here soon to remove the collar and deal with it," Luke said. "For now, we need to clear the area."

An agent took Gaither's arm to escort him away. "Good luck, Erin," the older man called.

She swallowed. "Thank you." But she couldn't help thinking she had used up her share of luck a long time ago.

After Gaither left the silence closed in around her. Luke walked some distance away to make a phone call. She closed her eyes and tried to pray, but her mind was a blank. All she could think of was Mark, of the joy on his face when he had been reunited with his daughter, of his bravery in fighting off Duane, of how tenderly he had touched Erin when they had made love.

"I've been talking to headquarters about your situation." Luke Renfro was beside the Jeep again. Being with him was a little disconcerting, he looked so much like Mark—though a Mark from a different world than the one they had shared. "We discussed getting a welder or someone like that up here to cut the collar off, but our explosives experts believe it's possible the device is set up to trigger with any kind of tampering," he said.

"Yes, Duane told us it was."

"We're still trying to find an explosives team that's closer," he said. "We aren't giving up yet."

She nodded. "I appreciate that."

"For now, we have to wait. And I'm going to have to leave you alone for a bit." He looked rueful. "I have orders to stay back at least eighteen hundred feet."

"I understand."

He took a step back, but she couldn't help calling out to him. "Agent Renfro? Luke?"

"Yes?"

"I didn't have anything to do with Duane Braeswood's awful plans," she said. "He was my stepfather, but I never saw him as anything but a madman and a criminal. Maybe I was wrong not to go to the authorities with what little I knew about him and his organization, but I was trying to protect my mother. And myself, too."

"You never gave us reason to believe you were guilty of any wrongdoing." He put his hand over hers on the door frame and squeezed it. "We're going to do everything we can to save you," he said. "I'll have my brother to answer to if I don't."

He walked away, leaving her to wonder what he had meant by that last statement.

Chapter Sixteen

The FBI had commandeered a local community center two miles from the park as their temporary headquarters. Mark had elected to go there with Mandy, instead of the emergency clinic, wanting to stay close to the action in case Erin needed him. Not that there was anything he could do, but he didn't want to be traveling in an ambulance somewhere, or knocked out on an operating table, if Erin asked for him.

One of the agents showed father and daughter to a room furnished with two folding chairs and a cot. Mark sat on the cot with his daughter, marveling at the feel of her in his arms. "You've gotten so big," he said.

"You're growing a beard." She rubbed her hand across the whiskers on his cheek.

"I haven't had time to shave lately," he said.

"I kind of like it." She snuggled against him. "Do you think Erin will be all right?"

His stomach tightened. "I hope so."

"She's very pretty." Mandy looked up at him from beneath her lashes. "Do you like her?"

"Yes, I like her."

"Are you in love with her?"

How was he supposed to answer that question? If he said yes, would Mandy think he was betraying her mother? Or worse, that he was turning his back on her? "Would you be upset if I said yes?" he asked.

"I think it would probably be okay. As long as I get to come live with you."

"Of course you'll live with me. You're my daughter and I love you very much." He kissed the top of her head. "So much."

"I love you, too, Daddy." She pressed her head against his chest. "Aunt Claire told me you might be dead, but I never believed her. I wouldn't let myself."

"I wouldn't have blamed you if you did," he said. "You had to wait a long time."

"It doesn't matter now that you're here."

They didn't say anything for a long while, and her breathing slowed and deepened. She had fallen asleep. Poor thing was probably exhausted. Later, he'd ask her what had happened with Duane and his men, though he wasn't sure he was ready to hear those details yet. Maybe he would find a counselor to help her deal with all the trauma of the past months. For that matter, maybe he would find someone to talk to himself. No telling what demons the events of the past months would leave him fighting.

He eased Mandy off his lap and laid her out on the cot. He was just standing when the door to their room opened and Luke stepped in.

"Why aren't you with Erin?" Mark demanded. Pain squeezed his chest. "Has something happened? Is she all right?"

"Nothing has changed." Luke set a brown paper bag on one of the folding chairs. "Did you go to the clinic about your arm?"

"I'll go later. Another hour or two isn't going to make any difference."

"I figured you'd say that, so I brought you some food. I thought you might be hungry."

Mark turned away. "I can't eat. Not until I know she's safe."

"We found an explosives guy who works for La Plata County," Luke said. "He's on his way."

"So you just left her alone?" Anger tightened his chest.

"There are two officers keeping an eye on her."

"But they're not with her. They don't know her. She's having to deal with this by herself."

"Mark, you know we can't risk any more lives."

His head told him Luke was right, but his heart screamed that the only life that really mattered was Erin's. "What does Braeswood say about the bomb?" he asked.

"Which one?" Luke opened one of the bags and began to set out burgers and fries. "He's already shut up and lawyered up. When he's not ranting about all the followers who will carry on his work even while he's in custody, he's reminding everyone that he is a frail old man who has suffered greatly and he's threatening to sue us."

"What about those followers?" Mark asked. "Did you arrest any of them?"

"Half a dozen or so. It was easy enough for our team to pick them out of the crowd. We've had some of them on our radar for months. But so far they're not talking, either. We're looking for more." He slid a cardboard tray of chicken nuggets toward Mandy, who had awakened and now perched on the edge of the cot. "Here you go, honey," he said. "Why don't you take these over by the window and eat while I talk to your dad."

Mark waited until Mandy had carried her lunch across the room before he spoke again, keeping his voice low. "Do you think Duane's right?" he asked. "When he says others will carry on his work?"

"I don't know. The world is full of crazies. We just try to stay one step ahead of them. We checked out the house you told us about, but it was clean. We figure he wasn't there but a couple of hours. Any other ideas where we might look for this alleged nuclear bomb?"

"There's a cabin in the mountains where he kept me and Erin prisoner. I think I could find it again, but he's probably cleaned it out by now. The last time I saw the trunk with the decoy in it, two of Duane's thugs were loading it into the back of a Hummer."

"When was this?" Luke asked.

"Two days ago."

"He could have driven or flown the trunk anywhere in the world by now."

"I'm telling you, it's not armed. It's all a bluff."

"You can't know that." Luke held up a hand

to forestall any further argument from Mark. "Even if the thing isn't a nuclear device, you can fit a pretty powerful explosive charge into a trunk like the one you described. So we don't have any choice but to take his threat seriously."

"I'm not saying you shouldn't take him seriously," Mark said. "Just that the man is a liar."

"Which we already knew." Luke slid a burger and fries toward Mark. "Eat this. You must be starving."

His stomach heaved at the thought of eating anything. "I can't eat. I can't stop thinking about Erin. I'd be dead now if it wasn't for her."

"You said she helped you escape. How?"

It wasn't so much what Erin had done, but what she had motivated *him* to do. "She created a distraction and I threw acid on one of the guards. Then we ran."

"When was this?" Luke asked.

"Two days ago. We got away while two of the guards were preoccupied with loading the trunk."

"You've spent two days wandering around out there?" Luke glanced out the window.

"We spent two days running from Duane's men." He glanced toward Mandy, who was sitting in the other chair, lining up her chicken nuggets in neat rows on the cardboard tray. "I killed three of them," he said softly. "And wounded another—not counting the man with the acid."

"We'll want a statement from you later." He handed Mark a cup of coffee. "I ought to warn you there are some people who want to make it hard for you because you cooperated with Braeswood and made the bomb he's threatening everyone with."

"I didn't cooperate with him!"

Mandy stared at him, her eyes wide. Mark forced himself to lower his voice and stay calm. "I didn't have any choice," he said. "And I didn't make a bomb. I made a fake to try to placate him."

Luke put a reassuring hand on Mark's shoulder—the uninjured one. "I'm pushing hard against any attempt to prosecute you," he said. "I've pointed out to anyone who will listen that you and Erin have cooperated fully. And you're the man who finally stopped Duane Braeswood. That's going to weigh heavily in your favor."

Mark stared into his coffee cup. "You caught the man, but you haven't really stopped anything. He's still threatening to put a big hole in the world with his supposed nuclear device.

He's still trying to kill Erin." He squeezed the cup the way he wished he had squeezed Duane Braeswood's neck, not caring that hot coffee sloshed onto his hand and splashed on the floor.

Luke studied him for a long moment. "How long have you been in love with her?" he asked.

Mark set the crushed cup aside and raked a hand through his hair. "I don't know. Maybe about five minutes after I met her." Anguish tore at him. "I never told her, though."

"You'll get a chance to tell her," Luke said.

Mark glanced toward Mandy, who was singing softly to herself as she dipped the chicken nuggets in ranch dressing and popped them into her mouth. "This is a lousy time to start a relationship," he said. "I don't want to upset Mandy."

"Mandy's a resilient little girl. And that's what counselors are for—to help with transitions like that. If you love Erin, you should try to make it work with her. Don't pass up a chance for happiness."

"What would you know about it?"

"You might be surprised." He sipped his coffee. "I'm engaged. To a journalist I met in Denver when we first came to Colorado on this case."

"Really? Congratulations." Mark began to pace. Hard to imagine Luke—the brother who had always been the sworn bachelor—finally settling down. Mark looked forward to the day when his own life was settled once more. He would never take the ordinary pleasure of living for granted again. But mundane routines seemed very far away right now. "When is this bomb guy supposed to get here?" he asked.

Luke's phone chirped. "That may be him now." He turned to leave the room, but Mark followed him out into the hall. "Go back to Mandy," Luke said.

"I'm coming with you," Mark said.

"And what happens when Mandy realizes you're not with her? Your daughter needs you, Mark. Let me take care of Erin."

Mark fisted his hands. How many times had he heard of someone being torn over some decision? Now he knew what that really felt like—a physical pain as if he was being ripped in two. He dragged in a ragged breath. "All right. But you'll bring her to me when this is over?"

"I will." They didn't say "if it works out all right" or "if she's still alive." But the words hung in the air between them, as real and horrifying as if they had been spoken.

ERIN FOCUSED ON a fly crawling across the dashboard, trying to shut out the sights and sounds outside the Jeep—the bright yellow police tape encircling the park with its ominous warning, Danger, Do Not Cross. Law enforcement officers from several agencies had closed off the streets leading to the park and shouted through bullhorns for people to clear the area. Luke had stopped by again a while ago to ask if she wanted anything to eat or drink, but she had refused. "I don't think I could swallow," she said.

He had nodded, his eyes full of real concern, but then he had left and she hadn't seen him again, or spoken to anyone. She was the queen bee at the center of a hive of activity, but unapproachable and dangerous.

She wondered what Mark and Mandy were doing right now. Maybe they were eating a good dinner, or taking a nap. Maybe father and daughter were merely catching up on the months they had lost, relearning each other again. She was glad Mandy had warmed to him so quickly. Her aunt must have done a good job of keeping the girl's memory of her father alive—or maybe Mark himself had been such a strong presence in her life before his disappearance that he wasn't easily forgotten.

A siren's blare jerked her from her reverie, the strident wail rising and falling and rising again as it drew near. She turned to watch a sheriff's department SUV turn in at the entrance to the park, idling a moment while officers scurried to move aside barriers, then pull up next to her.

A man dressed in something resembling a space suit stepped out, a tool bag in one hand, what looked like a small black safe with a handle attached to the top in the other. He saluted his driver, then the vehicle backed out and men moved the barriers back into place. The uniformed man made his way to the open driver's side window of the Jeep. "You must be Erin," he said.

"Yes."

"My name's Chad." He offered a hand and she shook it. "I'm here to deal with that rather unique necklace you're wearing." He tilted his head to study the device more closely. "What can you tell me about it?"

"Um, it's a bomb. With a timer. It's gold plated." She shrugged. "I don't know a lot."

Chad opened the Jeep's door. "Why don't you step out here and we'll get to work."

When she was standing in front of him, he set his tool bag on the front seat of the Jeep and opened the main compartment. "How much time does it say we have left?" she asked.

"Almost ten minutes." He placed the tip of a probe against the collar and watched the readout on a handheld monitor.

She swallowed. "Is that going to be enough?"

"I guess it had better be. Now hold still while I check this out."

She pressed her lips together, fighting the jittery nerves that made her want to scream. How could he be so calm and methodical as the seconds ticked down?

He removed a laptop computer and opened it on the seat next to the tool bag. He connected a handheld scanner to the computer and glided it slowly over the collar, studying the monitor display as he did so.

"It's okay to breathe," he said after a moment. "A good idea, actually."

She hadn't realized she had been holding her breath, and let it out in a whoosh. "Can you tell anything about the bomb?" she asked.

"I can tell a lot." He set aside the scanner and pulled out a bulky black helmet with a full-face visor. "You'll need to put this on," he said.

She gaped at him. "I don't really see the point. If this thing goes off, it's going to take my head clean off. I doubt a helmet will do much good."

The face mask on his own helmet prevented her from seeing his expression, but his voice remained calm and reasonable. "Right now, the helmet is to protect your eyes," he said. "I'm going to fire a laser at the collar. Oh, and you'll need to hold really still. I wouldn't want to miss the collar and hit you instead."

Meekly, she donned the helmet. Chad removed something that looked remarkably like a laser pointer from his tool bag. "Okay, close your eyes and lean your head back."

Before she could ask why she needed to close her eyes, he said, "You're less likely to flinch if your eyes are closed. The light is really bright."

She closed her eyes, leaned her head back and waited.

And waited. She could hear Chad breathing, and a bird singing somewhere behind her. The rumble of a distant truck engine. A small buzzing sound.

"Okay, lean forward a little."

She did as he asked and he moved behind her. She felt something pulling at her throat and then a cool breeze washed over her as he removed the collar. She opened her eyes and stared at him. "You did it," she said.

Though she couldn't see his face, she imagined him grinning. "The laser stopped the clock mechanism," he said. "We still have to disable the armament, but we can do that somewhere else." He opened the small safe, dropped the bomb inside and slammed the door shut. "All right, let's get you out of here." He reached up to remove her helmet.

But he had scarcely laid his hands on her when the bomb exploded, shattering the world and sending them flying.

Chapter Seventeen

The explosion shook the building where Mark and Mandy were waiting, rattling the chairs and knocking a painting of a sailboat on a lake to the floor, where it rested crookedly against the baseboard.

Mandy screamed and clung to her father. "What was that noise, Daddy?"

"I don't know," he lied, picking her up and walking to the window. It took all his willpower to stay on his feet and not give in to the sick dread that swept over him at the idea that the explosives experts hadn't gotten to Erin in time.

The cacophonous wail of multiple sirens filled the air, and car after car raced past the community center, headed toward the park. "Daddy, you're squeezing me too tight," Mandy said, pushing against his chest.

"Sorry, honey." Mark set his daughter down and moved to the door. A man raced past and Mark grabbed his sleeve. "What happened?" he asked.

"Somebody said a bomb went off in the park."

"Was anyone hurt?"

"I don't know. I'm going to find out." He pulled away and raced out of the building.

Mark wanted to follow him, but he couldn't leave Mandy here and he couldn't expose her to the carnage that might await at the park. He spotted a phone on a desk across the room and crossed to it. His fingers shook as, for the second time that day, he dialed his brother's number.

You have reached the voice mailbox of Special Agent Luke Renfro. Please leave a message at the tone.

Mark slammed down the phone and moved to the door, which the other man had left open in his haste to leave. An ambulance raced past, siren screaming. "No," Mark muttered. Then louder, "No!" He hadn't found love again only to have it torn from him.

A black SUV turned into the parking lot and parked in front of the door. Luke slid from the driver's seat, his expression grim. A dark streak that might have been blood painted the side of his face, and one sleeve of his coat was torn.

Mark gripped the door frame and watched his brother approach. Luke didn't say anything at first, merely pressed something into his hand.

Mark looked down at the cell phone. "What's this for?"

"So you can call me when you get to the emergency clinic."

Mark tried to hand back the phone. "I told you, I'm not going to the clinic. My injury can wait. What about Erin?"

Luke shoved the phone and a set of keys into Mark's hand again. "You're going to the clinic to see Erin. Go. The address is already programmed into the GPS. If you leave now, you'll get there just after the ambulance."

"Are you telling me Erin is alive?"

"Yes. And the bomb tech, too. He had already removed the necklace and placed it in a containment device when it blew. They were knocked off their feet, but they were both wearing helmets and he had on a bomb suit. He managed to shield her from most of the debris. The ambulance is taking them to the hospital as a precaution. The doctors will probably release them in an hour or two."

"How did you get this?" Mark touched the streak of blood on Luke's face.

Luke touched the spot and examined his fingers. "A sign fell on one of the sheriff's cars and trapped an officer inside. I helped pull it off and I guess I cut myself. Now go. I'll look after Mandy."

Mark clapped his brother on the back, then sprinted for the car.

"I'M FINE, REALLY. Most of these bruises are from before the explosion." Erin tried to fend off the probing hands of the emergency room physician and see past him to the next cubicle. "Is Chad okay?"

"I'm fine!" called a familiar voice. "Aren't you glad I made you wear that helmet?"

"Yes, thank you. And thank you for getting that necklace off me before it blew."

"My timing could have been a little better," he said. "I'm still trying to figure out what I did wrong."

"As far as I'm concerned, you did everything right. Ouch!" She flinched as a nurse sank a needle into her arm.

"Just a tetanus shot," the woman said. "Then you'll be free to go." She pressed a bandage over the injection site.

"No, I am not a relative. Not yet anyway."

Erin's heart leaped at the sound of the familiar voice. She stood and was moving toward the door when it burst open and Mark stepped inside. Their eyes locked and she hesitated, not sure how to read the expression there. "What are you doing here?" she asked. "Why aren't you with Mandy?"

"Luke is with Mandy." He moved toward her, but made no move to touch her. "I had to make sure you were okay."

"I'm fine." She smoothed her hands down the front of her shirt. "Hungry and dirty and a little banged up, but I'll be fine. How are you?"

"Same as you."

"How's Mandy?"

"She's good. Amazing."

"She is amazing. You're a very lucky man."

"Yeah. If you had said that a couple of weeks ago, I would have laughed in your face, but now I know I am lucky. I have a lot to be thankful for." He took her hand, and she sensed he was about to say something important—something she was afraid would hurt too much to hear.

"Luke, I…" she began.

"Mark Renfro?"

The man who joined them in the middle of

the emergency room had taken the cliché of the black-suited FBI agent and given it a twist—from his gelled, close-cropped black hair to the skinny trousers and slim-lapelled jacket of his black suit and his hipster skinny tie. "I'll need you to come with me, sir."

Mark frowned at the man. "You're interrupting a personal conversation."

"I'm sorry, sir, but your brother, Special Agent Renfro, sent me here to fetch you." He held up a badge and nodded to Erin. "You, too, miss."

Mark pulled Erin closer to his side and faced the interloper. "Who are you?"

"Special Agent Cameron Hsung." He moved the badge closer so that they could clearly see the official photo and credentials. "We need to go now. We don't have much time."

"Time for what?" Erin asked.

"I'll explain in the car."

"No." Mark turned away. "Tell Luke if he wants me he can come get me himself. I have more important things to do right now."

"Sir, if you won't come with me willingly, I have orders to bring you by force," Agent Hsung said. "This is a matter of life and death. Literally."

Erin slid her hand from Mark's. "What's going on?" she asked.

The agent glanced around the crowded emergency room. Every eye was focused on the trio in the center of the room. "Come outside," he said.

Mark and Erin followed him outside. He waited until the three of them were in his car before he said, "Duane Braeswood is threatening to set off his bomb in ten minutes if the president doesn't announce his resignation on national television. He says he can detonate it remotely, the same way he set off the bomb necklace in the park."

"How can he do that if he's in custody?" Erin asked.

"It's another bluff," Mark said. "The necklace probably had a secondary timer or other device that triggered if it was removed from your neck. There wasn't anything like that on the dummy bomb I built. And it's a dummy. It can't blow up." But he heard the doubt in his voice—doubt planted by Luke, who had pointed out that the bomb didn't have to be a nuclear device to maim and kill. And the exploding necklace Duane had fastened to Erin's neck proved the terrorist leader had at least one more explosives expert at his beck and call.

"You're among the few people who have ever seen this dummy bomb," Agent Hsung said. "We need you to help us figure out where the bomb might be, and positively identify it once it's located."

"And we need to do this in the next ten minutes," Erin said.

The agent glanced at his phone. "Eight minutes and fifty-four seconds now." He leaned forward and punched on the car radio.

"As law enforcement officials search frantically for a nuclear bomb that suspected terrorist Duane Braeswood claims will detonate in a matter of minutes, the president is preparing to meet with reporters in a live press conference. Previously, the president has stated he will not comply with Braeswood's call for his resignation and the resignations of his entire cabinet. Braeswood, leader of an extremist fringe group calling themselves the Patriots, is in FBI custody at this time, but has refused to reveal the whereabouts of the alleged nuclear device."

Mark's eyes met Erin's. "Where would Duane stash the bomb?" he asked.

She put a hand to her head, which ached from the aftermath of the explosion and from racking her brain, trying to figure out what Duane was up to. "He would want it nearby, I think," she said. "He couldn't have put it wherever it is by himself—he had to have people move it for him. At least two people."

"We're doing a house-to-house search in Doloroso right now," Hsung said. "But we're running out of time."

"Did you check the white panel van he was in?" Mark asked.

"The bomb's not there," Hsung said. "Though some evidence suggests it was at one time."

"And it's not at the house where he was staying?" Erin asked.

"We took the place apart. It's not there."

Mark pinched the bridge of his nose. "So he probably had the bomb in the van with him when he came to Dolorosa," he said. "He hid it somewhere after he got here."

Hsung turned to Erin. "You grew up in his house. You probably know him better than any of us. What would be his idea of a good place to plant a bomb? We've already ruled out the school and the county offices. We're running out of time."

"You're not running out of time," Mark said. "The bomb isn't real and Duane Braeswood knows it."

"That's right," Erin said. "He doesn't have to worry about putting the bomb where it will do the most damage. He could put it anywhere. It doesn't even matter if someone finds it after he gets what he wants from the government."

"No offense, but the rest of us aren't convinced the bomb is as dead as you say it is," Hsung said.

Erin felt a charge of inspiration. "That's it," she said. "It's a dead bomb." Her eyes met Mark's.

"The cemetery," they said in unison.

"Go to the Pioneer Cemetery," Erin told Hsung.

Hsung put the car in gear with one hand and hit a button on his phone with the other. "Get a team over to the cemetery," he said. "Erin thinks Braeswood might have put the bomb there."

The Pioneer Cemetery covered five acres at the south end of Doloroso, the site marked by an elaborate wrought iron archway, and towering lilac bushes poking their snow-covered bulk above a dry stack rock wall encircling the burial ground.

Hsung, Erin and Mark piled out of the agent's car as two armored vehicles pulled in behind them. "Where's the bomb?" the first man out of the first vehicle demanded.

"We don't know," Erin said. "We have to

look." She studied the scattered monuments and markers studding the snow-speckled grass, from the moss-covered weeping angels marking the graves of infants to a black marble obelisk in honor of some long-ago dignitary. But no shining metal trunk stood out among the plastic flowers and gravestones.

She started down the broad graveled path that led into the interior of the cemetery, Mark at her side, while the officers scattered through the rest of the grounds. "If we weren't on such an urgent mission, this would almost be pleasant," she said as they passed under the arching branches of a cottonwood, the bark silvery against the winter-blue sky.

"If there are any Braeswoods buried here, Duane might think it a good joke to deposit the bomb there," Mark said.

"He wouldn't know about that ahead of time," she said. "Wherever he put the bomb, it would have to be someplace he could get to easily, but away from the front gate, where anyone passing could spot it. I'm thinking back here." She gestured toward a rear section of the grounds. "The markers over there look older. Maybe the graves are less visited." She studied the rows of weathered wooden crosses and leaning granite stones. Then her gaze rested on a plump Cupid, the quiver of arrows on his back worn blunt from years of wind and weather. "There!" She pointed toward the Cupid. "Let's try there."

They spotted the trunk when they were approximately twenty yards from the marker, sun dappling its shiny metal surface where it sat in the middle of the sunken mound of the old grave. Mark hurried toward it, one hand outstretched. He had almost reached it when a voice behind him shouted, "Stop!"

Erin turned to see Agent Hsung striding across the ground between the gravestones. "Get back," he said. "Let the explosives techs take care of that."

Mark sent the agent a stubborn look, but stopped, then retraced his steps to rejoin Erin and Hsung. The agent led them back to the entrance to the cemetery, where they waited while a trio of bomb techs encircled the trunk.

"What made you think he'd put the trunk there?" Hsung asked.

"The Cupid," she said. "Duane has always had a very twisted view of love."

A shout rose from the trio by the grave, and they turned to see them standing with arms raised. Agent Hsung's phone rang and he put it to his ear and listened. "You were right," he told Mark. "The bomb was a dud. All show but no guts."

"That sort of describes Duane," Mark said.

Hsung pocketed his phone. "You two are free to go for now," he said. "Though stay close. We'll probably have some questions for you later."

"I don't have plans to go far." Mark took Erin's hand. He led her away from Hsung and the others, to the far end of the cemetery, beneath the snow-covered lilacs. "We didn't get to finish our conversation earlier," he said.

She tensed and tried to pull her hand from his, but he held tight. "You probably want to get back to Mandy," she said. "You two have so much to catch up on."

"We'll have time." He stopped and turned toward her, forcing her to stop, too. "I was saying before that I have a lot to be thankful for, and one of the things I'm most thankful for is you."

She looked away, her heart breaking a little as she did so. "Mark, don't," she began.

"Don't what? Tell you that I love you? Too late."

"Your daughter needs you right now. You both need time to heal. I would only be intruding."

"You're right. We all need to heal. But you're

wrong when you say I don't need you. I do. And Mandy needs you, too. She likes you. I think the three of us could make a family."

"How do you know she likes me?"

"She said she did."

"She might not like me as much if she thinks I'm taking you away from her."

"I thought you were done being afraid."

Erin had to look at him then. "What are you talking about?"

"That sounds like fear talking to me. You're afraid to take a chance with me and Mandy."

"I am not." Was he calling her a coward, just because she was trying to be sensitive to the feelings of a little girl who had lost her mother and almost lost her father?

"Then prove it," he said. "Show me you're not afraid to acknowledge your true feelings."

"All right, I will." She grabbed his face in her hands and stood on her toes to kiss him, a long, fierce kiss that left no doubt about her feelings for him.

He wrapped his arms around her and returned the kiss, moving from her mouth to her throat. "I was terrified when I heard that explosion," he whispered. "I thought I had lost you and never had a chance to tell you—to show you—how much I love you."

"I love you, too," she murmured, reveling in the feel of his lips gliding over her neck. "And I know I'll love Mandy, too."

Mark raised his head to look at her. "Does this mean you'll give us a chance?"

"Yes." She grinned. "If only to prove to you I'm not a coward."

"I never thought you were a coward," he said. "To me, you'll always be the bravest woman I know."

"Only because you showed me how brave I could be."

They kissed again. Pressed tightly to him, she felt something vibrate in his pocket. "What's that?" she asked, drawing away.

He pulled out the phone and frowned at the screen. "My brother." He hit the button to answer the call.

"Did you ask her yet?" Luke's voice was clear.

"Ask me what?" Erin asked.

"Did he ask you to marry him?"

"I'm working up to that," Mark said. "Give me a chance." His eyes met Erin's. "Would you?"

"Would I what?"

"Would you marry me?"

"What about Mandy?" she asked.

"I'm thinking a long engagement will give her time to get used to the idea."

Erin pulled him to her again, to whisper in his ear, "Yes."

"What did she say?" Luke's voice sounded a long way off as Mark returned the phone to his pocket.

"You and I have a lot of catching up to do," Mark said as he kissed her again.

"Mmm. And a lifetime to do it." In a way, they were both starting over, building new lives where love replaced fear, and neither of them ever had to be alone again.

* * * * *

LARGER-PRINT BOOKS!

HARLEQUIN

Presents®

PASSION
GUARANTEED
SEDUCTION

GET 2 FREE LARGER-PRINT NOVELS PLUS 2 FREE GIFTS!

YES! Please send me 2 FREE LARGER-PRINT Harlequin Presents® novels and my 2 FREE gifts (gifts are worth about $10). After receiving them, if I don't wish to receive any more books, I can return the shipping statement marked "cancel." If I don't cancel, I will receive 6 brand-new novels every month and be billed just $5.30 per book in the U.S. or $5.74 per book in Canada. That's a saving of at least 12% off the cover price! It's quite a bargain! Shipping and handling is just 50¢ per book in the U.S. and 75¢ per book in Canada.* I understand that accepting the 2 free books and gifts places me under no obligation to buy anything. I can always return a shipment and cancel at any time. Even if I never buy another book, the two free books and gifts are mine to keep forever.

176/376 HDN GHVY

Name	(PLEASE PRINT)	
Address		Apt. #
City	State/Prov.	Zip/Postal Code

Signature (if under 18, a parent or guardian must sign)

Mail to the Reader Service:
IN U.S.A.: P.O. Box 1867, Buffalo, NY 14240-1867
IN CANADA: P.O. Box 609, Fort Erie, Ontario L2A 5X3

Are you a subscriber to Harlequin Presents® books
and want to receive the larger-print edition?
Call 1-800-873-8635 today or visit us at www.ReaderService.com.

* Terms and prices subject to change without notice. Prices do not include applicable taxes. Sales tax applicable in N.Y. Canadian residents will be charged applicable taxes. Offer not valid in Quebec. This offer is limited to one order per household. Not valid for current subscribers to Harlequin Presents Larger-Print books. All orders subject to credit approval. Credit or debit balances in a customer's account(s) may be offset by any other outstanding balance owed by or to the customer. Please allow 4 to 6 weeks for delivery. Offer available while quantities last.

Your Privacy—The Reader Service is committed to protecting your privacy. Our Privacy Policy is available online at www.ReaderService.com or upon request from the Reader Service.

We make a portion of our mailing list available to reputable third parties that offer products we believe may interest you. If you prefer that we not exchange your name with third parties, or if you wish to clarify or modify your communication preferences, please visit us at www.ReaderService.com/consumerchoice or write to us at Reader Service Preference Service, P.O. Box 9062, Buffalo, NY 14240-9062. Include your complete name and address.

HPLP15

LARGER-PRINT BOOKS!

GET 2 FREE LARGER-PRINT NOVELS PLUS
2 FREE GIFTS!

♦HARLEQUIN®

Romance

From the Heart, For the Heart

YES! Please send me 2 FREE LARGER-PRINT Harlequin® Romance novels and my 2 FREE gifts (gifts are worth about $10). After receiving them, if I don't wish to receive any more books, I can return the shipping statement marked "cancel." If I don't cancel, I will receive 4 brand-new novels every month and be billed just $5.09 per book in the U.S. or $5.49 per book in Canada. That's a savings of at least 15% off the cover price! It's quite a bargain! Shipping and handling is just 50¢ per book in the U.S. and 75¢ per book in Canada.* I understand that accepting the 2 free books and gifts places me under no obligation to buy anything. I can always return a shipment and cancel at any time. Even if I never buy another book, the two free books and gifts are mine to keep forever.

119/319 HDN GHWC

Name	(PLEASE PRINT)	
Address		Apt. #
City	State/Prov.	Zip/Postal Code

Signature (if under 18, a parent or guardian must sign)

Mail to the Reader Service:
IN U.S.A.: P.O. Box 1867, Buffalo, NY 14240-1867
IN CANADA: P.O. Box 609, Fort Erie, Ontario L2A 5X3
Want to try two free books from another line?
Call 1-800-873-8635 or visit www.ReaderService.com.

* Terms and prices subject to change without notice. Prices do not include applicable taxes. Sales tax applicable in N.Y. Canadian residents will be charged applicable taxes. Offer not valid in Quebec. This offer is limited to one order per household. Not valid for current subscribers to Harlequin Romance Larger-Print books. All orders subject to credit approval. Credit or debit balances in a customer's account(s) may be offset by any other outstanding balance owed by or to the customer. Please allow 4 to 6 weeks for delivery. Offer available while quantities last.

Your Privacy—The Reader Service is committed to protecting your privacy. Our Privacy Policy is available online at www.ReaderService.com or upon request from the Reader Service.

We make a portion of our mailing list available to reputable third parties that offer products we believe may interest you. If you prefer that we not exchange your name with third parties, or if you wish to clarify or modify your communication preferences, please visit us at www.ReaderService.com/consumerschoice or write to us at Reader Service Preference Service, P.O. Box 9062, Buffalo, NY 14240-9062. Include your complete name and address.

LARGER-PRINT BOOKS!
GET 2 FREE LARGER-PRINT NOVELS PLUS
2 FREE GIFTS!

HARLEQUIN

super romance

More Story...More Romance

WESTERN WP PROMISES

YES! Please send me **The Western Promises Collection** in Larger Print. This collection begins with 3 FREE books and 2 FREE gifts (gifts valued at approx. \$14.00 retail) in the first shipment, along with the other first 4 books from the collection! If I do not cancel, I will receive 8 monthly shipments until I have the entire 51-book Western Promises collection. I will receive 2 or 3 FREE books in each shipment and I will pay just \$4.99 US/ \$5.89 CDN for each of the other four books in each shipment, plus \$2.99 for shipping and handling per shipment. *If I decide to keep the entire collection, I'll have paid for only 32 books, because 19 books are FREE! I understand that accepting the 3 free books and gifts places me under no obligation to buy anything. I can always return a shipment and cancel at any time. My free books and gifts are mine to keep no matter what I decide.

272 HCN 3070 472 HCN 3070

Name   (PLEASE PRINT)

Address   Apt. #

City   State/Prov.   Zip/Postal Code

Signature (if under 18, a parent or guardian must sign)

Mail to the **Reader Service:**

IN U.S.A.: P.O. Box 1867, Buffalo, NY 14240-1867
IN CANADA: P.O. Box 609, Fort Erie, Ontario L2A 5X3

* Terms and prices subject to change without notice. Prices do not include applicable taxes. Sales tax applicable in N.Y. Canadian residents will be charged applicable taxes. This offer is limited to one order per household. All orders subject to approval. Credit or debit balances in a customer's account(s) may be offset by any other outstanding balance owed by or to the customer. Please allow 4 to 6 weeks for delivery. Offer available while quantities last. Offer not available to Quebec residents.

Your Privacy—The Reader Service is committed to protecting your privacy. Our Privacy Policy is available online at www.ReaderService.com or upon request from the Reader Service.

We make a portion of our mailing list available to reputable third parties that offer products we believe may interest you. If you prefer that we not exchange your name with third parties, or if you wish to clarify or modify your communication preferences, please visit us at www.ReaderService.com/consumerchoice or write to us at Reader Service Preference Service, P.O. Box 9062, Buffalo, NY 14240-9062. Include your complete name and address.

WPBPA16R